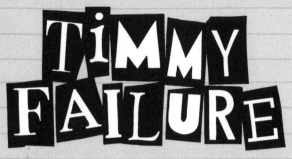

TIMMY FAILURE

IT'S THE END WHEN I
SAY IT'S THE END

STEPHAN PASTIS

CANDLEWICK PRESS

Copyright © 2018 by Stephan Pastis
Timmy Failure font copyright © 2012 by Stephan Pastis

First U.S. paperback edition 2019

Library of Congress Catalog Card Number 2018959551
ISBN 978-1-5362-0240-3 (hardcover)
ISBN 978-1-5362-0910-5 (paperback)

19 20 21 22 23 24 BVG 10 9 8 7 6 5 4 3 2 1

Printed in Berryville, VA, U.S.A.

This book was typeset in Nimrod.
The illustrations were done in pen and ink.

Candlewick Press
99 Dover Street
Somerville, Massachusetts 02144

visit us at www.candlewick.com

Visit www.timmyfailure.com
for games, downloadables, activities,
a blog, and more!

To my cousin Nick Tripodes, who never could have guessed when he drew this odd Santa in a Christmas card that I would steal it and use it in a book.

A Cliff-hanger of a Prologue That Will Make You Want to Read More of the Book. Also, It Contains a Giant Chicken.

Some kids start their day eating a complete, balanced breakfast.

I start mine trying to throw a principal out a window.

A window that is ten stories high.

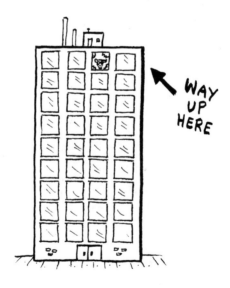

WAY
UP
HERE

I should have known it would end up like this when they wouldn't let me into the bar.

Even after showing my ID.

So I subdue the bouncer with a mix of

charm and martial arts and kick open the double doors of the bar.

Where I am accosted by two thugs I recognize: Rick "Drill-A-Kid" Drillashick and Crispin "Bowling Turkey" Flavius.

"Listen, boys," I tell them. "It doesn't

have to go down this way. I'm just here for a drink."

But they refuse to listen.

So I hurl them down the surface of the bar like they are human bowling balls.

And take my seat at the now-empty bar. Cool as the unopened beer bottle poised menacingly above my head.

"Dr. Alfredo Goni," I mutter, tapping my fingers on the shiny bar. "I should have known they'd throw an orthodontist at me."

"Right-o," he answers menacingly. "And I brought backup."

I whip around and see his accomplice.

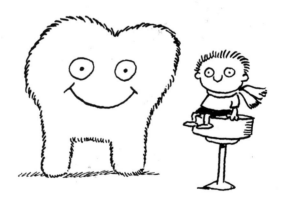

"I don't want any trouble," I tell Mickey Molar.

It is a tense moment. And nobody moves.

Except the grizzled bartender, who waddles toward me from behind the bar.

"Whaddya want?" she asks.

"Whiskey, neat," I tell her. "And don't try anything funny, Toots."

But she ducks. And my eye catches the quick flash of a beak in the mirror. And I spin around.

"Edward Higglebottom the Third!" I cry, hopping off my barstool. "I must say, I wasn't expecting a giant chicken."

And in a flash, the bar explodes in a frenzy of violence.

Punches. Kicks. Chicken feathers.

And one by one, I hurl a series of would-be assassins from the high window.

Ron "Speedo Steve."

"Minnie the Magnificent" Benedici.

Donny "Dangermouse" Dobbs.

And I make a run for the billiards room,
crashing through the makeshift barricade.

And I enter the dark, dingy room.

Where, brandishing a cue stick, is my school principal, Alexander Scrimshaw.

"We meet again," I tell him.

"Now look what you've done," he answers, surveying the damage to the bar.

"Mistakes were made," I tell him. "But none of them mine."

"Yeah, well, to get to me, you're gonna

have to go through the Scrum Bolo Chihuahua," he says, pointing to a giant Chihuahua perched atop the barroom light.

So I offer the Chihuahua a doggy treat.

And he licks my hand and runs off.

"I expected more," says Scrimshaw.

I watch as Scrimshaw backs farther away, waving the pool cue like a club.

"All we wanted was world domination," he says, "but you stood in the way. You, Timmy Failure. So I had to crush you. With algebra you'll never use. Pop quizzes you didn't expect. Boring novels you couldn't endure."

"I know," I answer. "And all under the guise of being a school principal."

"Yes."

"So what were you, really?" I ask.

"A secret agent for a vast criminal organization. All school principals are."

"Of course."

"So do what you will," he says. "But you won't take me alive."

"This could get ugly," I tell him.

"Principals like ugly," he answers.

And when I turn briefly to check for more of his goons, he kicks me behind the knees, sending me reeling.

As I struggle back onto my feet, he runs for the double doors. I spring like a cougar onto his back.

And from high atop his shoulders, I grab

him by both ears, steering him into the bar, the tables, the walls.

Dazed from the impact, he falls to the ground.

And I drag him to the broken window and lift him high overhead.

"Wait, wait, wait," he says, gasping for breath. "I will make you a deal."

"I am about to vanquish my enemy forever. There is nothing more I could want."

"But there is."

"Then talk fast," I tell him. "Because you're very heavy. Portly, even."

"Next Tuesday," he says, "there will be a pop quiz in geography. Spare my life and you don't have to take it."

"Will I still get a good grade?"

"B," he answers.

"A minus," I say.

"B plus," he counters.

"Deal," I say, putting him down.

And when I do, he shoves me with both hands.

And I fall through the window.

Where my shoelace snags on the window frame.

And my life hangs by a thread.

"You fiend," I utter as I dangle like the pendulum of a clock.

"It's the end of Timmy Failure," he says, bending down to cut the shoelace with a piece of broken glass.

"It's the end when I say it's the end," I tell him.

And he cuts the shoelace.

"Okay, now it's the end," I say.

And I fall.

But not before leaving him with some final words of wisdom:

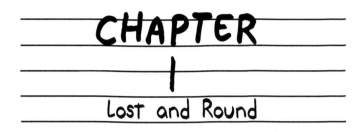

CHAPTER 1

Lost and Round

"Did he look like this?" I ask my polar bear, Total, as I show him the sketch I've drawn.

0802451

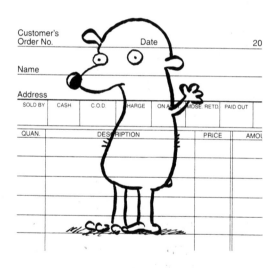

"Sorry about the paper," I add. "It was the only thing I could find in the house."

Total stares at the drawing.

"But does it look like him?" I ask.

He shakes his head.

Smaller, he indicates with his paws.

As a detective trained in forensic drawing, I have had to sketch my fair share of individuals. But rarely have I had a client this fussy.

"Like this?" I ask, showing him another drawing.

0802452

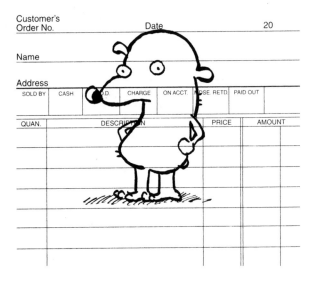

Rounder, he indicates with his paws.

"Like this?" I ask again. "Is this what your big brother looked like?"

0802454

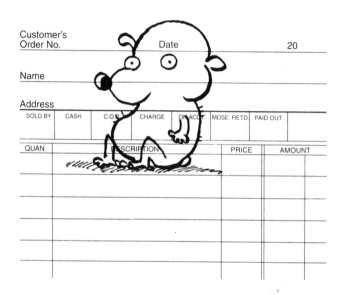

Customer's Order No.			Date				20	
Name								
Address								
SOLD BY	CASH	C.O.D.	CHARGE	ON ACCT.	MDSE. RETD.	PAID OUT		
QUAN.		DESCRIPTION				PRICE		AMOUNT

And suddenly, my polar bear is quiet.

He pulls the drawing out of my hands and carries it a few yards away.

Where he sits on the grass and stares at it. Like it is his actual brother in his hands.

I have known for years that my polar bear grew up without a mother somewhere in the Arctic.

But it was not until the two of us watched a nature documentary about two polar bear cubs that something in his furry brain was jarred loose.

A memory.

One that was buried deep under an unusually large Arctic snowdrift that separated him from his brother.

Forcing my polar bear to go it alone.

As he's remained to this day.

"If you want me to help you reach him,

I will," I tell him. "But first we have to find him."

Total continues staring at the sketch.

"It would be a substantial disruption of my normal detective business," I explain. "But I feel obligated."

But he remains silent. For he is a bear. And bears are not good at expressing emotion.

So I sit down on the grass beside him and wait.

Hoping for a sign on this bright, cloudless morning.

And then the sun disappears.

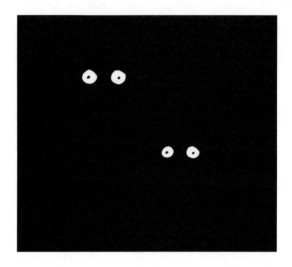

CHAPTER 2

Total Eclipse of the Smart

"Timmy, it was a solar eclipse," says my best friend, Rollo Tookus.

ROLLO TOOKUS

Stanfurd

"Wrong, Rollo Tookus," I answer. "It was much more than that."

"Class," announces our teacher, Mr. Jenkins, "before we get started, I'd like a show of hands. How many of you were able to see the eclipse this morning?"

My classmates raise their hands.

"And did you all use the special dark glasses?" asks Mr. Jenkins.

"I used them," answers Molly Moskins, still wearing the glasses.

"You can probably take the glasses off now, Molly. You're indoors."

"Is that where I am?" she replies. "I can't see a thing."

"All right," continues Mr. Jenkins, "which of you would like to come up and briefly explain to the class what a solar eclipse is?"

"I will," volunteers Corrina Corrina, a former detective and current has-been who there is absolutely no reason to talk about.

FORMER DETECTIVE. CURRENT HAS-BEEN. →

"Great," says Mr. Jenkins. "Go for it."

She walks to the front of the class.

"A solar eclipse is when the moon passes in front of the sun," she says.

"Very good," comments Mr. Jenkins.

Rollo raises his hand.

"Yes, Rollo?"

"I knew all of that," he volunteers.

"I bet you did," answers Mr. Jenkins.

"Will it be on the final?" asks Rollo.

"Rollo, relax," says Mr. Jenkins.

"Because I didn't take any notes," adds Rollo.

"Okay," says Mr. Jenkins, "let's all —"

"Mr. Jenkins," I say, raising my hand, something I have done only four times this semester, three of which were to ask:

"Yes, Timmy," says Mr. Jenkins. "What do you want?"

"I'd like to say more about the solar eclipse we saw this morning."

As I have never volunteered for one academic exercise in the history of my education, my teacher is momentarily stunned.

"Okay, Timmy. Sure. But make it brief."

I walk to the front of the class and climb atop Mr. Jenkins's chair.

"What you saw this morning was a sign from the gods," I announce.

No one speaks.

"And, thus, I hereby retire from the detective business."

CHAPTER 3

Heavens Can't Wait

The news of my retirement stuns my classmates, sending them into a dazed stupor that is visible at recess.

But there is nothing I can do to help them.

For my decision is final.

"Want to play kickball with the rest of us?" Rollo asks me.

"It'll be okay, Rollo," I remind him. "We'll still be friends and I shall still be attending school."

"What are you talking about?" he asks as a stray kickball rolls past us.

"My retirement," I remind him.

Max Hodges runs past us to chase the ball.

"You will all be okay," I tell Rollo. "For my spirit shall be with ye unto the end of time."

Max overhears us.

"You really are a weirdo," he says.

I wait until he is gone. "Keep your voice down, Rollo. Spies abound."

"Yeah, well, I didn't really get the whole retirement thing," Rollo says. "I mean, what does an eclipse have to do with your quitting the detective business?"

It's moments like this when I realize that a 4.6 grade point average is really quite meaningless.

"Okay, Rollo, if I have to lay it out, I will," I say, sighing.

"Okay, but hurry up. I want to go play."

"Don't rush me, Rollo," I reply, pointing toward my bear behind the fence. "Because this is about the big guy."

"God?"

"Total," I answer. "But, yes, the gods also."

"I don't understand."

So I try again.

"Rollo, my polar bear informed me that he needed my help. But I hesitated, because I knew the strains it would put on my detective business, both in terms of time and money. And caught in this moral quandary, I looked to the heavens."

"And?"

"And the sun disappeared from the sky."

"Yeah. The moon covered it."

"No," I answer. "I think it exploded."

"Timmy, if the sun exploded, why is it back in the sky now?"

"Well, I'm not a physicist," I explain, "but it must have un-exploded."

Rollo just stares.

"The point is that the heavens spoke to me, Rollo. And they said, 'Timmy, ye must retire.'"

"Okay," says Rollo. "I'm gonna go play now."

So off he runs.

And I use the rest of recess to write my memoirs.

CHAPTER
4
Memoirs Light the Corners of My Mind

AUTHOR'S NOTE:
AS STATED, MY GOAL UPON RETIRING WAS TO HELP MY BEAR. BUT SINCE RETIRING, I HAVE BEEN HOUNDED BY SCHOLARS AND CRIME-FIGHTING PROFESSIONALS TO COMMIT MY LIFE'S STORY TO PAPER IN ONE COMPREHENSIVE VOLUME. THUS, HERE IS A BRIEF SYNOPSIS.

MEMOIRS

I am Failure. Timmy Failure.
I am the founder, president, and
C.E.O. of the detective agency I
have named for myself, Failure, INC.
(Well, I was all those things. Before
I retired 30 minutes ago.)

I have solved all of the world's most
notorious crimes, which are so numerous
that I must crowd them into one
tiny footnote.[1]

---

1. The case of the stolen Segway;
The case of the missing Halloween candy;
The case of the missing Spooney Spoon;
The case of the missing globe;
The case of the stolen nature report;
The case of the stolen YIP YAP funds;
The case of the missing Rollo;
The case of the missing captain's money;
(And, yes, I could have saved space by
not repeating the words "THE CASE OF"
over and over. But it's too late now.
Also, why are you reading the
footnotes?)

I solved all these crimes with very little help from my former business partner, Total.

Total, the polar bear you saw earlier.

I say "Former" because our business relationship has been something less than stable. Specifically, Total has:

- Become a partner in the agency;
- Been forced from the agency;
- Rejoined the agency;
- Quit the agency;
- Rejoined the agency;
- Been on probation with the agency;
- Been fired from the agency;
- Rejoined the agency;
- Been demoted by the agency;
- Fled to Cuba.

But Total is not the only individual causing personal strife in my life.

There is also my mother, who married the former doorman of our apartment building, Doorman Dave, thereby making him Husband Dave.

MOTHER   HUSBAND DAVE

The three of us were supposed to move to Chicago for Husband Dave's job, but that didn't happen.

So now we live together in a townhouse they bought downtown. And if you're wondering what a townhouse is, here is my best explanation:

I don't know

Lastly, there is also my father, who I met for the first time last summer:

FATHER

(CAN'T REMEMBER WHAT HE LOOKED LIKE, SO I DREW A MAN'S SHOE.)

And now, I am retired from the detective business.

And though content, I am fearful that criminals will use this opportunity to once again ply their trade.

Thereby plunging the world into chaos.

A fate much too horrible to

CHAPTER
5
Hat Trick

"You interrupted me in the middle of my writing," I inform my teacher, Mr. Jenkins. "And you seized that without a warrant."

"Timmy, you got back from recess a half hour ago and you haven't looked up from your desk once," he says, glancing at the documents he has grabbed. "And what is this you're writing, anyway?"

"Please do not look at that. It's highly confidential."

"Fine," he says, handing the pages back to me. "But, Timmy, you need to pay attention and not be working on your own stuff."

"I can do both."

"Okay," says Mr. Jenkins. "What have we been talking about for the last thirty minutes?"

"The solar eclipse," I answer.

"That was *before* recess."

"Well, then I have no idea. Perhaps you're jumping from topic to topic too rapidly."

"I can help him," interrupts Rollo, handing me a document.

"What is this?" I ask.

"What he's been talking about," says Rollo. "The big project for the semester."

So I peruse the document.

CREATIVE ASSIGNMENT

All the students in the class will work together on writing, directing, and producing a film that is to be no less than 30 minutes in length.

Each student's role will be assigned randomly.

Enjoy!

"WHAT?" I cry. "I have no time for a stupid film."

"You said you're retired now," answers Mr. Jenkins. "So you have plenty of time."

"I'm retired to do *other* things," I tell him. "Like help my polar bear. And write my memoirs."

"And work on a film," replies Mr. Jenkins, pointing to his desk. "Now, go pick a job out of the hat like Nunzio and everyone else."

"I get to do lighting!" shouts Nunzio Benedici, pulling a piece of paper out of the hat. "I guess I just turn the lights on and off!"

"Well, it's a little more involved than that," says Mr. Jenkins. "But it is relatively easy."

"I'm craft services!" shouts Rollo, pulling his hand from the hat. "Wait. What's that?"

"You bring the food," answers Mr. Jenkins.

"My mother is the greatest cook ever!" exclaims Rollo. "Will I be graded on her macaroni and cheese?"

"Perhaps," answers Mr. Jenkins. "If she brings enough for me."

"Absurd!" I cry, pointing at Rollo and Nunzio. "Rollo just has to eat pasta, and Nunzio's gonna turn off the lights when he's done. How fair is that?"

"Stop complaining, Timmy, and reach into the hat."

So I reach into the hat to pick a job.

"With your eyes *closed*," says Mr. Jenkins.

So I reach into the hat again, this time with my eyes closed.

And grab a slip of paper.

And suddenly, my retirement is ruined.

Writer of the entire movie

CHAPTER
6
Boy Interrupted

"How am I supposed to write an entire movie?!" I yell to my mother that night.

"Hush," she says, "I'm trying to watch TV."

So I stand in front of the TV to get her attention.

"What in the world are you wearing?" asks my mother.

"It's my smoking jacket and pipe," I answer. "Given that I am now retired from detective work, I am supposed to be a man of leisure."

"Where'd you get that pipe?"

"Husband Dave gave it to me."

"No, I didn't," says Husband Dave, seated beside her on the couch. "He must have taken it from my sock drawer."

"Give me that," she says, taking the pipe from my mouth.

"You are no help at all," I tell Husband Dave.

NO HELP AT ALL

"Timmy, we have a whole extra bedroom in this townhouse," says my mother. "It's quiet. It has its own computer. Just go in there and write. Because the two of us would like to watch this film."

"Looks boring," I say, glancing at the screen. "What is it?"

"It's about a big, fancy ship that hits an iceberg," says my mother. "And there's a man and a woman and they fall in love and they kiss."

CHAPTER 7

Titanic Failure

The next day at school, I turn in my proposed film synopsis.

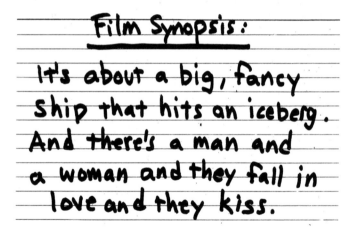

Film Synopsis:

It's about a big, fancy ship that hits an iceberg. And there's a man and a woman and they fall in love and they kiss.

"Timmy," says Mr. Jenkins, "you just stole the plot from the movie *Titanic*."

"Artists don't steal," I reply. "They *borrow*."

"Yes, but you stole."

"Fine. What if I change it slightly and have the boat hit an elephant?"

"How did elephants get into the ocean?"

"Parachuted from airplanes," I answer.

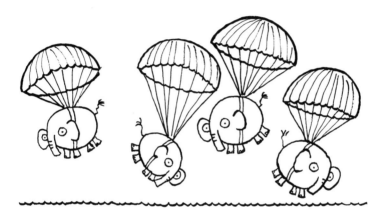

"Timmy, you have to come up with your own idea," says Mr. Jenkins. "That's all there is to it."

"But I'm a detective, not a writer! We don't write stories—we ARE the story!"

"Yeah," he says, leaning back in his chair and putting his feet on the desk.

"Yeah, what?" I answer.

"You said you wanted to write your memoirs, right?"

"Right."

"Well, instead of doing that, why not turn them into a film?"

CHAPTER 8

A Timmy Is Born

"I have never seen you work so hard on anything in your life," says my mother, peeking into my writing hovel, formerly known as the extra bedroom.

"Mother, I'm in the midst of a particularly compelling piece of dialogue. And the muse is a fickle master. Please. Give this writer space."

She reaches down and lifts a page of my screenplay from the floor.

"Wow," she comments.

"Which draft are you reading?" I ask.

"This one," she says.

```
INT. HOSPITAL ROOM - AFTERNOON

The MOTHER of our hero is about
to give birth in a hospital.

But it is not the usual kind of
birth.

For TIMMY FAILURE is descending
into the world on the wings of
flying elephants.

There are 600 elephants.
```

"That's the first scene," I tell her.

"That's quite an entrance."

"Yes," I answer. "My problem now is that

the screenplay is limited to one hundred pages. And my birth sequence alone is seventy-five pages."

"Maybe you can cut out some parts."

"No. It's all inspired work. So nothing can be deleted."

"Well, I'm glad you're excited about it. But just five more minutes, okay? You have school tomorrow and I don't want you to be exhausted."

"Got it."

"Five minutes," she says. "Promise?"

"Promise."

CHAPTER 9

The Ebbs and Flos of Filmmaking

"I stayed up all night writing this," I proclaim to my classmates, all gathered together at the city library for our film project meeting. "And it is a masterpiece."

"Not sleeping is bad for your health," says Molly Moskins. "You could have died."

"I know," I answer. "But sometimes that's the price of art."

"I don't want to die," says Rollo Tookus. "I just want to get an A."

"I should tell all of you one thing right now," I continue. "And that is that I plan on running a very tight ship on this film. So if any of you are less than fully committed to my vision, you should probably leave now."

Angel de Manzanas Naranjas rises and heads for the door.

Angel de
Manzanas
Naranjas

"Where are you going?" I ask.

"I'm not even partially committed," he says.

The library door slams behind him.

"None of you saw that," announces Toody Tululu, hopping to her feet.

"Why not?" asks Nunzio Benedici, seated next to her.

"Because I'm in charge of publicity on this film, and we can't have the world finding out that the production is already falling apart."

"Nothing is falling apart," I remind them. "I have everything under control."

"Can we talk about costs?" asks Corrina Corrina. "Because I'm the producer and I have to see to it that we don't spend more than the nine hundred dollars Mr. Jenkins is giving us."

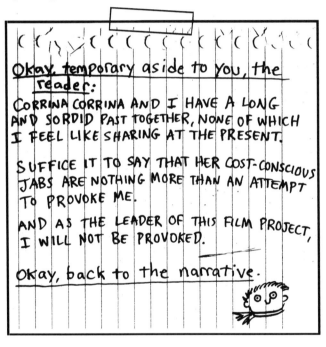

Okay, temporary aside to you, the reader:

CORRINA CORRINA AND I HAVE A LONG AND SORDID PAST TOGETHER, NONE OF WHICH I FEEL LIKE SHARING AT THE PRESENT.

SUFFICE IT TO SAY THAT HER COST-CONSCIOUS JABS ARE NOTHING MORE THAN AN ATTEMPT TO PROVOKE ME.

AND AS THE LEADER OF THIS FILM PROJECT, I WILL NOT BE PROVOKED.

Okay, back to the narrative.

"None of you are going to worry about costs," I say without looking in Corrina

Corrina's direction. "The bar scene alone will cost ten times that."

"What bar scene?" asks Rollo.

"I walk into a bar filled with mobsters, and one by one I throw each of them out a tenth-story window."

"The actors could die," interjects Molly. "I vote that nobody dies in this film."

"No one is gonna die," I remind her. "Because we have trained stuntmen."

"Who?" she asks.

"Max Hodges," I tell her.

"I'm not a trained stuntman," interrupts Max.

"You will be," I assure him.

"No, I won't," answers Max, standing up.

"Because I'm going home."

Max opens the library door and leaves.

"Fine," I answer. "We'll just make Gunnar or Jimmy Weber or Nunzio the stuntmen."

"No way. I'm in charge of lighting," says Nunzio, springing from his seat and turning off the lights.

We are momentarily in darkness.

When the lights are turned back on, Gunnar and Jimmy Weber are gone.

"Oh, God," says Toody Tululu. "This whole thing is a disaster."

"There will be no talk of disasters," I announce. "You will all be proud to say you were a part of this film."

"I don't even know what it's about," says Scutaro Holmes.

"It's about a boy and his polar bear," I explain. "And you, Scutaro, are lucky enough to be playing the polar bear."

"Do I get to eat anyone?" asks Scutaro.

"Only the evil ogre."

"Who's the evil ogre?"

"Principal Scrimshaw," I explain.

"Timmy," interjects Rollo, "we can't make a film where a polar bear eats our school principal. We'll get a bad grade."

"Yes, well, if need be, I have a PG-rated version where the polar bear just chases Scrimshaw off a cliff and he falls to the valley floor."

(ARTIST'S CONCEPTION.)

"Then he better *bounce* off the valley floor!" yells Molly. "And live happily ever after."

"Okay," says a voice from behind us, "you guys are gonna have to keep your voices down."

We all turn to see the city librarian, Flo, standing behind us.

"I'm fine lending you kids one of our conference rooms to work on your film, but not if you're gonna be loud."

"Sorry, Flo," I tell him. "We're having artistic differences."

"But please don't tell anyone," adds Toody Tululu.

"All right, well, we're closing up anyway," says Flo. "You have two minutes."

"But, Flo," I plead, "I still have to explain my artistic vision. That'll take hours."

"Do it in two minutes," Flo says as he

walks out the conference-room door.

With Flo gone, I sit quietly, thinking of how I can cram my brilliant vision of the film into a mere two minutes.

And then a boy wearing a scarf speaks up.

"I don't need to hear your vision," he says. "I have my own."

John John, Total Con,
Went to School and
Now Fun's Gone

"I don't even know who you are," I say to the boy with the scarf after we both leave the now-closed library.

"Tom John John," he answers.

TOM
JOHN
JOHN

"What kind of a name is that?"

"What do you mean? My name is Tom, but that's my dad's name also, so my family calls me by my first and middle names put together, which is 'Tom John.'"

"But you said 'John' twice."

"Yes, 'John' is our last name also."

"That's quite odd," I tell him.

"Not as odd as forcing all of us to make a film about your life," says Tom John John. "Did Mr. Jenkins approve that?"

"Yes, he approved it," I inform him. "It was his idea. And if you'd like to contribute to the film, perhaps I could find you a job bringing me coffee or feeding the mules."

"Yes, well, I have a much different concept of our respective roles."

"Well, good for you, Tom John John, but I'm the writer, and when it comes to a film, there is nobody more important than the writer."

"Yes, there is," he answers.

"No, there's not," I reply.

As we argue, I see Rollo Tookus waiting for the bus to pick him up from the library. So I turn to him to break the tie.

"Hey, Rollo, tell this kid with the scarf who the most important person on a film is."

"The director," Rollo shouts over the rumble of his arriving bus.

"A director?" I yell back at him. "Who's ever heard of a director?"

"Mr. Jenkins explained it all to us," answers Rollo as he boards his bus. "But I think you were writing your memoirs."

"All right, fine," I shout. "Say there is such a thing as a director, what's he do?"

"He's in charge of the whole film," answers Rollo from his seat on the bus.

"The whole film?" I mumble as the bus

starts moving. "Then who's this clown?" I yell, pointing at Tom John John.

Rollo pokes his head out the window of the departing bus and shouts:

"He's the directorrrrrrr!"

CHAPTER
11
I Saw Mama Keeping
Stuff Because

"Tom John John is a transfer student," says my mother as we drive in her car. "I think one of the parents said his family hops around a lot. Mostly in Europe."

"So we can deport him," I tell her.

"Kick him out of the country? No, Timmy. We can't kick him out of the country."

"But he wears a scarf. It's very pompous."

"*You* wear a scarf, Timmy."

"Yes. And it makes me look quite distinguished. He, on the other hand, looks buffoonish."

DISTINGUISHED   BUFFOONISH

She stops the car in front of a storage facility.

"Is this where your storage unit is?" I ask.

"Yep."

"Why do we even have a storage unit?"

"Because when we moved out of our house, I had nowhere to keep the stuff from our garage," she says as she unlocks the padlock on the large metallic door. "Now, help me push this door up."

We push up the large metallic door and I
see a large array of boxes.

"This place is huge," I tell her. "Have you
thought about living in here?"

"No, Timmy. We have a nice home."

"Yeah, but what if Husband Dave gets on
your nerves? You could hide here."

"I'm not gonna hide in a storage unit,
Timmy."

"Well, maybe I should have a key. In case Husband Dave gets on *my* nerves."

"Are you gonna start looking through these boxes or not?" she asks. "You're the one who wanted to look for something."

It's true. I did.

And there, on top of a box, I find it.

CHAPTER 12

Just the Fax, Ma'am

It's a well-known fact that many advanced mammals can communicate over long distances.

For lions, it is a roar that can echo across canyons.

For whales, it is a tone that can carry for miles underwater.

And for polar bears, it is the fax machine.

Not much is known about how polar bears got their hands on so many fax machines. Some speculate that when people started discarding them in the 2000s, they were scooped up by polar bears posing as Goodwill truck drivers.

Though we'll never know for sure.

In any event, the way a fax machine works is this:

You stick a piece of paper into a machine that reads all the information on the paper.

Then you dial the fax number of whomever you want to send the document to.

Then, like magic, the other person's fax machine spits out an identical copy of your document.

At first, polar bears were confused by

the technology. They thought that when you stuck a piece of paper into a fax machine, it magically flew through the air to the other person's fax machine, the same as if you had just folded it up into a paper airplane and sailed it over to your friend.

As such, they tried to use it to send bologna.

Please don't put bologna in the fax machine.

But once they figured out the technology, polar bears created a vast network of communication capable of spreading news, sharing gossip, and finding relatives.

"This is how we're going to find your big brother," I explain to Total, holding the fax machine I got from my mother's storage unit.

He just stares at it.

"And we'll keep it here in my writing hovel, which will also serve as our headquarters for this top-secret mission."

"WHATT for short," I inform him.

Total is so happy, he hugs me.

"All right, let's not get emotional," I tell him. "I'm only helping you because we're professional colleagues."

He puts me back down.

"Now, this is what I'm going to be sending to everyone. Does it look okay?"

Total feels compelled to tack on a note of his own.

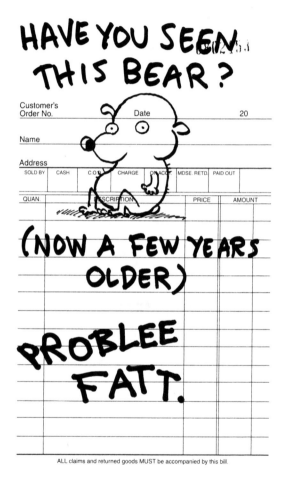

HAVE YOU SEEN THIS BEAR?

(NOW A FEW YEARS OLDER)

PROBLEE FATT.

"Good," I tell him. "Back in my detective days, I did a lot of missing-person cases. And

I can tell you that it's important to provide as much detail as you can."

I hand him another piece of paper, with the numbers 867 written across the top.

"This is the area code for most of the Arctic," I tell him. "Just start faxing as many random numbers with that area code as you can. Even if you don't find your brother, you'll surely find someone who's *heard* of your brother."

But before I can say more, my Mr. Froggie phone rings.

CHAPTER 13
Do You Hear What I Hear? A Fax, a Fax, Ringing in My Ear

"What are you doing calling on the Mr. Froggie phone?" I ask my best friend, Rollo Tookus.

"I tried calling you on your regular house phone," says Rollo Tookus. "But it made this really awful computer noise."

"Yes, well, that's because we're using it to send faxes to the Arctic."

Beep
Boop
Beep

"That sounds like something I don't want to know about."

"Correct. It's top secret."

"Okay, well, that's not why I called."

"Of course it's not. You called on the Mr. Froggie phone. And that's for clients only. But I've already told you I'm retired."

"I know, Timmy. You explained all that. But that's not why I called, either."

"Well, then spit it out, Rollo Tookus. I'm in the midst of a very critical mission and I have absolutely no time to spare."

"Fine, Timmy. I just called to tell you you're missing Elf-topia."

"I'll be right there," I answer.

CHAPTER

14

Elves to the Left of Me,
Rollos to the Right

Elf-topia is the largest gathering of elves on the North American continent. It occurs in the front window of Elmsley's, our city's lone department store.

There they gather, together with Santa Claus himself, who sits regally on his throne.

The highlight of the event occurs when one of the elves (Ernie Elf) escorts a live reindeer (Biscuit) to the foot of Santa's throne. There, Santa touches the nose of the reindeer, and when he does, it glows red.

And the spectacle is repeated throughout the Christmas shopping season, to the delight of the easily amused townsfolk.

But that's not why I came.

I came because last week Biscuit did not like having his nose touched and kicked Ernie Elf through the window.

It was, other than my own exploits, one of the most exciting things to ever happen in our town.

But, much like my career, it was not meant to last.

"Where is everybody?" I ask Rollo from in front of Elmsley's lifeless window.

ELMSLEY'S

"They canceled it. I think one of the elves is suing somebody."

"You brought me down here for *nothing*?"

"I'm really sorry, Timmy. I didn't find out until after I called you. But it's not for nothing. They're having piggyback races through the department store instead."

"Well, that sounds profoundly stupid."

"It's not. The winner gets a hundred-dollar gift certificate from Elmsley's."

"A hundred dollars?" I reply, aware that such a sum could bankroll a good chunk of my film, currently titled *Greatness on Two Shoes: The Timmy Failure Story*.

"Fine," I tell him. "I'll do it."

"Great," says Rollo Tookus, climbing up on his father's back. "Just get on someone's back."

"Whose?" I ask.

"Didn't you come here with your mom?"

"She had to work today, Rollo Tookus. Her law firm wanted her to finish something."

"What about Dave?"

"He's working also."

"On a Saturday?"

"He works for a hotel. They always work weekends."

"Well, then how'd you get here?"

"I *walked* here, Rollo Tookus. On two feet. One after another."

"Oh," says Rollo. "I just figured you came with somebody."

I look around the room and see the other kids, all of whom are on a parent's back.

"Well, how about you get on my dad's back instead?" he says.

"No, thanks," I say. "He's your dad."

So I look around to see if there is a spare parent.

But there is not.

"I don't have to race, Timmy. Really. Just ride on my dad's shoulders."

But there is no need.

For by the time he finishes saying it, I am already gone.

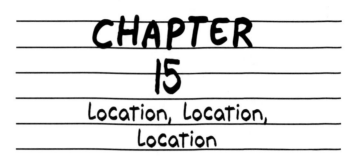

CHAPTER 15

Location, Location, Location

Gone because there is work to do.

Not detective work, despite the public's demand for me.

But film work.

Specifically, finding the locations where we will film *Greatness on Two Shoes: The Timmy Failure Story*.

So I search the lonely city streets.

For the high-rise that will be the head-quarters of Failure, Inc.

THE BIGGER, THE BETTER

For the boat that will take me to my island fortress:

For the blimp I will use to save the helpless townspeople.

But as I walk, I see only boring things.

Until I come to a bar. And remembering that there is a pivotal bar scene where I kick in the doors and hurl the mobsters out the window with brute force, I am intrigued.

"Well, it's not ten stories high," I think aloud, "but I suppose with a top-notch special-effects department, we can make it *seem* like it's ten stories high."

And fortunately for me, it has the kind of doors that can be easily kicked in.

So I do that.

And once inside, I see someone I recognize.

CHAPTER 16

The Keys to Success

"Dad?"

"Son! What are you doing here?"

"What are *you* doing here? I thought you were in—wherever that place is."

"The Florida Keys. But, yeah, had a bit of bad luck. My restaurant was flooded. Big hurricane."

"So you came here?"

"Yeah. I still have friends here from when your mother and me were together.

And one of them told me about a bartending job here. I just need it until I can get back on my feet. I was going to call you just as soon as I—"

"Say no more," I tell him. "I understand."

For my father is not a bartender. Or a restaurant owner.

He is an international secret agent who catches criminals.

Like his son.

INTERNATIONAL SECRET AGENTS

"I see great possibilities," I tell him as I walk the length of the seedy bar.

"Okay," he answers.

"Perhaps a crime-fighting partnership. I could even come out of retirement for it. Did you hear about my retirement?"

"I don't think I did."

"What? Don't they have newspapers in Florida?"

"Yeah. But I must have missed that."

A customer with a potbelly ambles into the bar.

"Give me a second, Tim."

My dad walks behind the bar and fills a frosted glass with beer.

I hop onto a barstool.

"It goes without saying," I tell my father, "but our partnership would have to be secret."

"Right," he says, handing the customer a bowl of peanuts.

"There are just too many people who want to off us," I remind him.

"Off us?"

"Eliminate us. You know, because we pose a threat to their crime-loving ways."

"Oh, right."

A man and a woman walk into the bar.

"Hey, son, I want to talk more about this, but you probably shouldn't be in here. It's sort of just for adults. But listen, if you're not doing anything next weekend, and your mom says it's okay, we can go to the park or something."

"Sure," I answer. "But not the park. Too risky."

ASSASSINS CAN BE HIDING...

"Fine," he says. "Well, you pick someplace. But I have to take care of these people."

"Right," I say, hopping off the barstool.

My dad pours a gold-colored drink into two tiny glasses.

"See you soon, buddy," he says as I walk toward the doors. "And if you need anything, just tell me."

So I stop. And turn around.

"I need your bar for a film."

CHAPTER

17

Where Do I Begin to Tell the Story of How Grating a Tom John John Can Be?

"Timmy, you have to compromise on this a bit," says Mr. Jenkins.

I am meeting with him after school. And Tom John John is sitting in the chair next to me.

Looking his usual self.

BUFFOONISH

"But Tom John John has no vision for the film," I complain to Mr. Jenkins. "I am the writer. I have the vision."

"Yes, well, he's the director," says Mr. Jenkins. "And he has a vision, too."

Tom John John nods.

"Tell him your vision, Tom John," says Mr. Jenkins. "And maybe the two of you can reach a middle ground."

"May I use your whiteboard?" he asks.

"Sure," says Mr. Jenkins.

"Well, to be as laconic as possible, I see the film like this," he says as he begins walking toward the board.

"I object!" I answer, rising to my feet.

"Object to what?" asks Mr. Jenkins.

"To the word 'laconic.' I think it means 'insulting.'"

"No, Timmy," says Mr. Jenkins. "It means 'brief.'"

"We'll see," I answer. "Because I'm pretty sure it will be insulting."

"Please sit back down," says Mr. Jenkins.

I sit back down.

Tom John John writes on the board.

"So basically," he says, "I see the film like this."

I fall out of my chair.

"Timmy," says Mr. Jenkins, "please sit in your chair and stay there."

I sit back in my chair.

"And there are two paramours vying for his love," continues Tom John John. "One of whom is Corrina Corrina."

I fall out of my chair again.

"Well, now, that's horrific," I cry from the floor. "And I don't even know what a paramour is."

"It's someone you're having a romantic relationship with," says Tom John John.

"Oh, good God," I mutter, wanting to fall again but already on the floor.

"All right, enough, Timmy," says Mr. Jenkins. "You and Tom John are just going to have to work it out. Explain your respective visions and agree on something."

"Fine," I answer. "Can I write on the whiteboard, too?"

"Sure," replies Mr. Jenkins.

"Okay," I say. "Here is my vision for the film."

"That's not really a vision," interrupts Tom John John.

"It's a very visionary vision," I reply.

"No," he argues. "A vision for a film has a compelling plot, good characters, surprising twists, and a solid ending."

"Fine," I answer, writing on the board again. "Here is my vision."

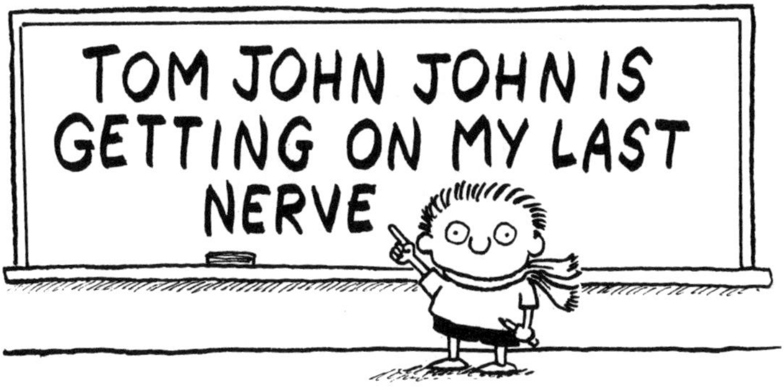
TOM JOHN JOHN IS GETTING ON MY LAST NERVE

CHAPTER 18

The Butterfly Effect

"He expects me to work closely with Corrina Corrina!" I shout to Rollo Tookus on our walk home from school. "And have her be my girlfriend!"

"It'll be fine," says Rollo. "The important thing is that we all try to get a good grade."

"Who cares about stupid grades!?"

"I do," says Rollo Tookus. "Because I want to get into Stanfurd. And get a good job. And not have to sell oranges by the side of the highway."

ROLLO'S WORST FEAR

Stanfurd

"Rollo, do I need to recite what that girl has done to me?"

"No. Please. You don't."

But I do.

So here you go:

Corrina Corrina was once the head of her own detective agency, the Corrina Corrina Intelligence Agency (CCIA).

It was corrupt, horrid, wretched, godforsaken, and bad.

It was also unfair, as her father was wealthy, and she exploited his vast resources to create a high-tech detective lab in her extravagant downtown headquarters.

And yet, despite all these advantages, my agency still crushed her like a Corrina Corrina butterfly on the windshield of life.

So she quit the detective business.

Which was wise.

Because she was always a criminal at heart, her crimes too numerous to list.

Though I will try:

Stealing Segways.[1]

Getting me kicked out of school.[2]

Looting school treasuries.[3]

Kidnapping my best friend.[4]

Spying on me in my vacation abode.[5]

---

1. *See* Timmy Failure, Book 1
2. *See* Timmy Failure, Book 2
3. *See* Timmy Failure, Book 4
4. *See* Timmy Failure, Book 5
5. *See* Timmy Failure, Book 6

And whenever I present this litany of offenses, Rollo feels compelled to add the following:

"Don't leave out that time you kissed her."[6]

"Listen to me," I say to Rollo Tookus as we stop on a street corner for the light. "I'm making this film my way. And as my best friend, you're gonna help."

"Not if it affects my grade," he answers.

"Even if it affects your grade!" I tell him.

But before I can argue, I see a polar bear fleeing.

---

6. *DON'T see* Timmy Failure, Book 3. Because it's a big lie. And it didn't happen.

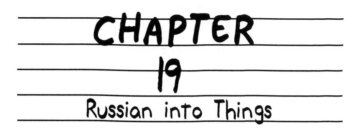

CHAPTER 19

Russian into Things

"Why are you getting on a bus?" I ask my polar bear, Total.

He holds out a sheet of paper.

"Someone found your brother!" I exclaim. "It's gotta be your brother! He shares all of your character flaws."

Total nods. The bus doors spring open.

"But you can't take the bus to Russia," I tell him. "There's a big ocean in between."

"You gonna board?" asks the bus driver.

I look at the driver briefly and then turn back to my polar bear.

"You don't even know where in Russia he

is," I say to Total. "It's a big place. And it has people with big hats."

BIG HAT

"Hey!" yells the bus driver. "You boarding or not?"

"No," I tell him. "He was just confused."

"Who was confused?" he asks.

"Never mind," I tell him. "You're interrupting a very personal conversation."

The driver just stares at me, then pushes the button that closes the automatic doors.

I watch as the bus roars off.

When I turn back to Total, he is sitting on

the bus-stop bench, his tiny suitcase resting at his feet.

And he is sad.

"And were you just gonna leave without saying good-bye to me?" I ask him. "That's not very businesslike."

I sit on the bench beside him.

"Besides, there are protocols for this kind of thing. Retirement parties. Gold watches."

I look at his wrist. It is much too big for a watch. Not to mention that he can't tell time.

"Well, maybe not a watch. But a party all the same."

I look up at him.

"The point is that our business relationship goes back many years. And something like that deserves to be celebrated."

He puts his fuzzy arm around me.

"I give you my word as the greatest detective in town—well, former detective," I correct myself. "I will find your brother."

CHAPTER 20

WHATT Bear Is This?

When we get home that Friday night, Total and I hunker down in WHATT and pursue the promising lead we have on his brother.

And slowly the layers of his brother's life are revealed.

Each of them dripping with tartar sauce.

"He keeps trying to rob the same Seafood Sammy's in Churchill, Manitoba," I explain. "All to get fish sticks."

Total shakes his head, then drools, caught halfway between disappointment and envy.

"And when the people in the restaurant see him coming, they lock the doors," I tell my polar bear. "Then he just stands there knocking and looking pathetic until the police arrive."

Total and I peruse the bear's rap sheet.

"He's been arrested thirty-one times," I say as we look through the photos taken by the restaurant's security camera.

Photos of the time he tried to act fierce.

Of the time he disguised himself as a unicorn.

Of the time he ran into a pole.

Total covers his eyes in shame.

"It is ironic that your brother has chosen a life of crime and you have chosen a life of law enforcement. You are like the yin and yang of polar bears. Forever balancing the universe."

But my profundity is lost on him.

And I can see that the story of his brother has made him sad.

So I watch as he exits WHATT.

And follow him through the townhouse.

Where I see the story has not made him sad.

But hungry.

CHAPTER
21
Dawn of the Dad

But the search for Total's brother is only one of many tasks filling my leisure years.

So on Saturday morning, I awake before everyone else to address another.

"I didn't even know this time of day existed," I say to my father, who is surprised to see me.

"Tim, it's six in the morning. We're not even open yet. What in the world are you doing here?"

"You said we could do something this weekend. So we're doing something."

My father unlocks the door.

"I meant father-and-son things, Tim."

"I see," I answer. "So what exactly are those?"

"Come inside," he says, shaking his head. "It's too chilly out here."

I follow him inside.

"Did you mention to your mother that you wanted to do something with me?" he asks.

"I believe so."

"And she was okay with that?"

"Almost certainly."

He glances back.

"Listen," he says. "When you go back home today, you tell her. I don't want her coming down on me for this."

"Yes, sir."

He walks around the bar, turning on one item after another: lights, neon signs, a slot machine, a jukebox. Slowly, the sleepy bar awakens.

"And do me a favor," he adds. "Don't mention you came to a bar. Tell her we met at a park or something."

"Yes, sir."

He begins removing clean glasses from a

small dishwasher and placing them in a rack overhead.

"And, hey, not for nothing," he says, "but one of the regulars mentioned to Ms. Dundledorf that I let a kid in here. So we need to be a little more careful."

"Who's this Dundledorf?"

"She owns the place. Not a friendly person."

DUNDLEDORF (NOT a friendly person.)

"Well, no need to worry. It's six in the morning. I doubt you'll have any customers."

But when my father opens the back door, there are customers. And like ghosts, they float wordlessly to their seats.

One of which I'm sitting in.

"Hey, what's this kid doing on my stool?" a man in a fedora asks.

"Tim, go sit in one of the booths," says my dad.

I watch as the man in the fedora rearranges everything on the bar in front of him. Taking a saltshaker and moving it to a table. Grabbing a table placard and moving it to the bar. Picking up a discarded newspaper and handing it to my dad to throw out.

"Fred's a little obsessive," says my dad as he walks past me to throw the newspaper in a recycle bin in the back. "Everything in its right place."

"And I thought *school* was filled with riff-raff," I comment. "This place is a zoo."

"Tim, I'll tell you what," my dad says. "Why don't I meet you somewhere tonight? After my shift."

"I can't. Mom says we have to do some family thing. It's quite frivolous. But I'll be here tomorrow morning at the same time."

"Well—"

"And take this," I tell him, handing him the large stack of paper in my hand, "so we can talk about it tomorrow."

"What is it?"

"The film I wrote for school," I answer. "You'd be well advised to pay particular attention to the bar scene. It will take place here."

"What are you talking about?"

"I told you about it last week."

"Are you crazy? I can't have a bunch of kids in here. It's bad enough I let you in."

"Don't worry. We'll do it when the place is closed. And my school will repay you for the broken windows."

"What broken windows?" asks my dad.

"The ones caused by the defenestration."

"The *what*?"

"Defenestration. The act of throwing someone out a window. It's the best word in the dictionary."

DEFENESTRATION

"All right, enough," he says. "No one's getting thrown out of windows."

"Yes, they are. Customers," I tell him. "Not yours, though. Stuntmen. Unless you *want* us to throw a customer out the window."

An older customer calls out for my dad. "Hey, you talking or bartending?"

"Coming," my dad tells him.

"Okay," my dad says to me, "you gotta go."

"Right. Be back tomorrow. Same time."

"No."

"Yes. It's the best time. More covert."

"No, Tim."

"Coffee!" interrupts the old man. "Black!"

"Here I come, here I come," my dad calls out to him.

"Tim," my dad says, leaning down to talk to me, "talk to your mother. Make sure seeing me is okay. And I'll call her later and work something out. But you're not filming anything in this bar."

The old man hops off his barstool and lands on his spindly legs.

"Okay," he says, marching toward us. "You want me to get the coffee myself? I'll get it myself."

And I catch his eye.

And he freezes like a toad before a Timmy train.

CHAPTER 22

Old Man Crocus, That Old Man Crocus, He Just Keeps Rolling Along

"Oh, good God," he says.

"Old Man Crocus," I mutter.

"Is there no place in this world that's safe from you?" he cries.

"You two know each other?" asks my dad.

"He was my teacher," I explain.

"He drove me out of the profession," replies Crocus.

"He was the best teacher I ever had," I explain.

"He caused me a nervous breakdown," replies Crocus.

"The profession wore him out," I explain.

"He crashed a car through my wall," replies Crocus.

"He took a well-earned retirement," I explain.

"I fled to Key West to escape him," replies Crocus.

I stop and stare at Crocus. "Wait. *You* were in Key West?"

My dad leaves to get Crocus his coffee.

"Yes, I was in Key West!" he barks. *"And I was happy!"*

"Until," he adds, raising a fist, "it all ended!"

His fist falls like a coconut upon the bar.

The man in the fedora looks our way.

"Goodness," I say to Crocus. "What happened?"

"I'll tell you what happened," he says, removing his wire-rimmed glasses and rubbing the bridge of his nose. "I was taking a stroll along the beach when I heard a shrill voice echoing out from on high."

"Oh, I know the feeling," I answer. "The gods spoke to me just recently."

"No, no, no," he says, his voice rising in tone. "This was no god. It was *you,* Timmy Failure, standing atop a lighthouse."

"Ah, yes," I reply. "I was surveying my domain."

"No," he says. "You were tracking me across the globe, like a demon on horseback."

"Oh my," I respond. "I like that image. Perhaps I can use it in my movie."

POSSIBLE MOVIE IDEA →

"Yes, well, I didn't like it at all," answers Crocus. "So I fled Key West. Moved back here to live with my brother. Figured I could at least hide from you in a bar. But no. Look. *You.*"

"Yes," I answer. "It feels like the gods have thrown us together for a reason. Perhaps you can play yourself in the film."

My dad hands Crocus his coffee. Crocus stares into the blackness.

"What's the matter?" asks my dad. "Not how you like it?"

And leaving his coffee on the bar, Crocus drifts off toward the double doors.

And stops.

"No," he grumbles through gritted teeth. "*Nothing* is how I like it."

And as he says it, the doors swing open. And we see an elf.

"Hey," says the elf. "Try getting kicked in the head by a reindeer."

CHAPTER 23

Here Comes Mama's Wrath, Here Comes Mama's Wrath, Right Down Santa Claus Lane

But the elf is not the only unhappy person this holiday season.

"Your father's in town and you went and saw him without even telling me?" asks my mother as she drives the car.

"I thought I told you," I answer from the backseat.

"I didn't hear you tell her," says Husband Dave, sitting in the passenger seat beside her.

"Please, Husband Dave," I reply. "No teaming up. It's bad enough with just one of you."

"And how exactly did you even know he was in town?" continues my mother. "Because he certainly didn't tell me."

"What do you mean how'd I know? I just found him."

"Where?" asks my mother, turning to look back at me.

"Driver's handbook says to keep your eyes on the road at all times," I remind her.

"Timmy, where did you find him?" she snaps.

"In a park!" I shout.

"Which park?!" she shouts back.

"The *Park Park*!" I yell, as though it's a proper name. "You know, the one with the grass."

My mother says nothing.

The mood grows tense.

And it is a mood at odds with the antlers on our heads.

"And if you don't mind," I say, breaking the silence, "how about someone telling me why we're all dressed like reindeer?"

Husband Dave turns toward the back-seat.

"We're caning the Moskins family."

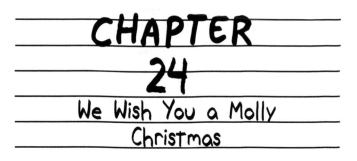

CHAPTER 24

We Wish You a Molly Christmas

Molly Moskins smiles too much and smells like a tangerine. Plus she has mismatched pupils.

MOLLY MOSKINS

MISMATCHED PUPILS

TANGERINE

She and I have had what I can only refer

to as an off-again, on-again relationship.

For I have partnered with her.

And arrested her.

As such, one can never be quite sure

what side of the law she is on. For she is a kid-size chameleon, steeped in treachery.

MANY DIFFERENT COLORS, BUT CAN'T SHOW YOU DUE TO TECHNOLOGICAL LIMITATIONS OF BOOK

But for all her faults and felonies, I find the notion of caning her excessive.

"We're gonna hit Molly with a cane?" I ask Husband Dave.

"Timmy, I told you all of this when we were at home," says my mother as she stops the car in front of Molly's house. "It's called candy caning."

"How is it any better if we hit her with a candy cane?" I ask. "Is it that she'll smell minty afterward?"

"Nobody's hitting anybody," says my mother, turning off the engine. "When you candy cane a house, you sneak up to it at night with a bunch of candy canes and hang them everywhere."

"Oh, good God," I utter. "This sounds like a tragedy in the making."

"Shhh, Timmy," says Husband Dave. "It's supposed to be a secret. You don't want her to hear us."

The two of them get out of the car. Guarding my bean, I follow.

"Mother, you do not sneak up on a sacred

abode at night," I whisper as we jog up the Moskinses' front lawn. "As a former detective, I can tell you that this whole neighborhood is heavily armed."

"Here, take these," she says, handing me a fistful of candy canes.

"And let me tell you something," I add. "When Mr. Moskins shoots us, he will be fully within his rights. Because we are now common trespassers."

As I issue cautionary proclamations, I spot Husband Dave foolishly approaching the front door and hanging a candy cane on the Moskinses' doorknob.

"Oh, great," I add. "Your husband has a death wish. And to think, he'll die in reindeer antlers."

But neither of them is heeding my warnings.

So I throw my candy canes and antlers to the ground and hide behind the large unlit Christmas tree in the center of the front yard.

Low to the ground.

Hands over head.

Prepared for urban violence.

But hoping to not be seen.

And then the Christmas tree lights up

like a Christmas tree.

CHAPTER 25

The Reindeer Hunters

"Nobody shoot!" I yell. "Mistakes were made!"

"Hey, put these back on," says Molly Moskins, towering over me. "They're adorable!"

I survey the scene. Assess the threat level.

"Tell me plainly," I say to Molly Moskins as I rise to my feet, "have my mother and Dave been taken hostage?"

"I don't think so," she says.

"Well, if they have, I'd like to negotiate for the release of my mother. You can probably keep Dave."

"I think your mom and dad are just inside having eggnog with my parents," she says, smiling broadly.

"Dave is not my dad, Molly Moskins. I have a dad. A very prominent dad with a background I don't wish to share. And he has generously volunteered his bar for a pivotal scene in our film."

"Oooh. Your dad owns a bar?"

"I've said too much already," I answer. "Suffice it to say that the scene will be made particularly engaging by the real-life grittiness of the setting."

"I see," says Molly, biting her lip. "I wonder if that's the place we kiss."

Sickened, I hold on to the Christmas tree for support.

"Molly, I assure you there are no kissing scenes in my script. None. Zero. Nada."

"Oh, I wasn't talking about *your* script," she answers. "I was talking about Tom John John's."

CHAPTER 26
Empty Chairs at Empty Library Tables

After school on Monday, I march into the city-library conference room like a detective possessed.

And find nobody.

"They left," says Flo, peering into the room. "About ten minutes ago."

"Well, why'd they leave?" I ask. "We're supposed to be having a film meeting here."

"I think it was the kid with the scarf. He thought the room was too confining. Said it didn't have the right, uh, *joie de vivre.*"

"What the heck is that?" I ask.

"You know, I'm not really sure myself," says Flo. "But I'd watch out for that kid. I don't think he likes you."

"We're mortal enemies," I explain. "I loathed him from the moment I saw him in that pretentious little scarf. I mean, who *wears* something like that?"

Flo stares at me.

"Enough chitchat," I continue. "I need intel, Flo. Where they went. How they got there. What the danger level is."

Flo looks from side to side to make sure no one is listening.

"It's very dangerous," he whispers.

"I can handle it," I tell him.

"Myrtle's Garden of Flowers," he says.

CHAPTER 27

If You're Going to Film Rehearsal, Be Sure to Wear Some Flowers in Your Hair

With Flo's help, I locate my enemy's secret lair.

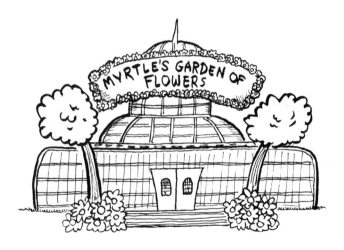

And it is indeed filled with flowers.
Each more dangerous than the last.

And inside, I spring upon the spineless coconspirators.

"So, a rehearsal without the writer!" I declare. "For shame."

I am approached by the conspiracy's ringleader.

"Relax, friend," says Tom John John.

"We are not friends," I answer. "We are at best awkward acquaintances."

"Well, then, awkward acquaintance, we just thought the rehearsal made a bit more sense here," he says. "Given that the film has a rather significant greenhouse scene where the characters' faces are framed by begonias and ducks."

"I see," I answer. "So a *joie de vivre* is a duck."

JOIE DE VIVRE

"*Joie de vivre* is not a duck," says Rollo Tookus, who is standing behind a table filled with food. "It means 'enjoyment of life' in French."

I stare at Rollo.

"French? This isn't a French film. And

what exactly are *you* doing here anyway?"

"It's an official movie meeting. I have to be here. For my grade. Want to try my mom's guacamole?"

I shake my head at Rollo. "You couldn't call and tell me about the new location?"

"I *did* call," says Rollo, "but I got that stupid computer sound again, and you told me the Mr. Froggie line is only for clients."

"Can we hurry up?" cries a muffled voice from behind us. "I'm melting in this stupid thing."

I turn around and see something that is best described as a cross between a polar bear and a sewing machine accident.

"It's me, Scutaro," says the sewing machine accident.

"What is *that* supposed to be?" I ask.

"A polar bear," says Corrina Corrina, our film's producer. "It was all we could afford."

"In the previews, we'll use clips of actual polar bears," says Toody Tululu. "Provided that's ethical."

"None of this is ethical!" I cry. "This whole thing is unethical!"

"Bravo! Bravo!" says Tom John John, clapping his hands slowly as he walks toward me. "Very dramatic."

I am tempted to pick him up and toss him into a flock of *joie de vivres*.

He smiles and stands beside me.

"Perhaps the *enfant terrible* can explain to all these eager souls what his vision for the film actually is."

I turn to Rollo. "*Enfant terrible.* Is that a chicken or a duck?"

"I think that refers to you," says Rollo, his mouth crammed with guacamole.

"Fine," I tell the entire cast and crew assembled around me. "You want to hear my vision? I'll tell you."

I pause for dramatic effect. And then commence with a flourish.

"Our film will open in a hospital, where our hero is born, a gift unto the world. It's compelling. Dramatic. And it will require six hundred flying elephants."

NAKED BABY TIMMY

FLYING ELEPHANT

"No chance," says Corrina Corrina. "We don't even have enough money for a hamster."

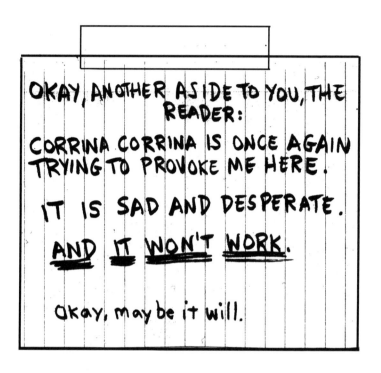

OKAY, ANOTHER ASIDE TO YOU, THE READER:

CORRINA CORRINA IS ONCE AGAIN TRYING TO PROVOKE ME HERE.

IT IS SAD AND DESPERATE.

AND IT WON'T WORK.

Okay, maybe it will.

"WILL YOU PLEASE SHUT YOUR PIEHOLE?" I yell in a professional way. "You know diddly-doodly about cinema!"

"I guess I don't know diddly-doodly about cinema, either," says our lighting director, Nunzio Benedici. "Because I don't get any of it. Who is this hero you keep talking about?"

I look over at Nunzio and see that he is passing time by shoving gravel up his nose.

"*I'm* the hero, Nunzio!" I answer. "Me! Timmy Failure!"

Nunzio shoves more gravel up his nose.

"Now, listen," I continue. "In act two of the film, we follow our defiant hero through his youth and watch as he slowly but methodically creates the world's largest detective agency. A beacon of hope in an otherwise grim world."

"That must be why I fall in love with him," says Molly Moskins.

"No," I interrupt. "There'll be none of that here. This film is gritty and raw."

Molly sighs.

"And that is because I am consumed by vengeance," I add. "For my polar bear and I are beset on all sides by enemies."

"Can I be one of your enemies?" asks Angel de Manzanas Naranjas, seated in the corner beside a banana plant. "Because I've never really liked you."

"No," I answer. "Because those roles have already been cast. But the point is that I attack them all, and in the process, I blow up a train station and survive a tsunami and throw forty men out of a tall building."

The cast and crew are speechless.

"All in 3-D," I add. "So make sure you put that in the budget."

"Nope," says Corrina Corrina.

"And by the way," adds Rollo, "if any of you enjoyed my mother's guacamole today, I'd appreciate you filling out one of these feedback forms. It can affect my grade."

Tom John John rubs his chin. "Thank you, Timmy, for that interesting concept. But it's not the film I'm making."

"It is now," I answer.

"Well, no, I'm the director. And I can assure you that the film I am making is not that. Mine will be black-and-white. Moody."

He holds out two pieces of paper.

"Read a couple pages yourself," he says.

```
INT. CAFE - NIGHT

Two young girls, both attractive, sit at
separate tables.

A boy enters.  He is sad, lonely, pathetic.
This is Timmy Failure.

                TIMMY
          My business is failing.  I am
          failing.

One of the two girls approaches his table.
She has black hair with a small bow.  Her name
is Corrina Corrina.

                CORRINA CORRINA
          Pardon me, sir, but I sense you have
          a whiff of failure about you.  Can I
          ask your name?

                TIMMY
          Failure.

                CORRINA CORRINA
          That is almost too ironic for words.

CLOSE-UP of sweat on Timmy's brow.  His
nervous hands. His pleading eyes.

                TIMMY
          Spare a dime for a muffin?
```

"Sad? Lonely? Pathetic?" I cry. "And I'm begging for food?"

"Yes," answers Tom John John. "But read on. Things improve markedly."

```
The girl at the other table approaches.  She
has curly hair and gorgeous eyes.  She is the
great Molly Moskins.

                    MOLLY
          Pardon me, but I couldn't help
          overhearing you. And I think I can
          help.

                    TIMMY
          With money for a muffin?

                    MOLLY
          No.  By rebranding you.  You are
          no longer Timmy Failure.  You are
          now Johnny Success.

                    TIMMY
          That is brilliant.

                    MOLLY
          I agree.

                    CORRINA CORRINA
          Yes.  And with her marketing help
          and my expertise in detective work,
          perhaps we can turn your life
          around.  For we are two powerful
          women. And you are but a soiled
          ragamuffin.

                    TIMMY
          Spare a dime for a ragamuffin?

They all hug.

Timmy gets on his knees.  Kisses their shoes.
```

"What is happening here?" I shout.

"Well, there's some wordplay involved. A ragamuffin is a child in ragged clothes, while a muffin is—"

"Who cares about muffins?" I reply. "This is character assassination! A world-class detective doesn't kiss anyone's shoes!"

"Okay, I am seriously gonna faint in this thing," interrupts Scutaro. "Can we discuss muffins and shoes later?"

"Well, I, for one, love what I've seen of Tom John's script," interjects Molly. "I think it makes Timmy more likable. Particularly later, when he falls in love with both Corrina Corrina and me, but each of us decides we don't want to be with him."

"*Merci,* Molly," replies Tom John John before turning to me. "And, Timmy, we may be able to compromise on that bar after all. Because at the end, we flash forward, and there you are, elderly and heartbroken and drinking milkshakes alone."

But before I can argue further, I hear a loud noise.

And see that it was caused by a polar bear.

Not the fake one fainting.

But the real one knocking.

CHAPTER 28

Greenland Acres Is the Place to Be

I rush outside to join him.

"What are you doing here?" I ask him.

Total holds out a fax.

From: Anonymous   Phone: Anonymous

Your brother is in a minimum-security prison in Nuuk, Greenland.

You didn't hear it from me.

The fax includes a photo of his brother's prison mug shot.

And judging by the photo, the prison truly is minimum security.

NUUK, GREENLAND

101668 6024

"He's trying to escape right in the middle of his mug shot," I comment. "He's even waving good-bye."

Total nods.

"Your brother's not wise," I tell him. "By now they've caught him and thrown him back in the clink."

I look at the last page of the fax and see that it includes the address of the prison.

"If this is accurate, it looks like we know right where your brother is," I tell my polar bear.

Who, when I look up, is already holding his suitcase.

"Whoa, whoa, whoa," I caution him. "Before you do anything, you need to write to your brother first. He may not remember you at all. So explain who you are. Your whole history. Be as detailed as you can."

Total takes a moment to write on the back of the fax.

"Needs more detail," I say to him. "Tell him as much as you can."

Total tries again.

"I don't even know what that means," I tell him. "Are you calling *him* fat or you?"

Total nods.

"Okay, we can work on your letter later. First we should plan your route to Greenland. I think it's an island, so the transportation planning could get quite complex."

Total writes on the back of another page.

"Swim?" I shout. "It's thousands of miles. You get tired just walking to the refrigerator."

Total nods again.

"Sounds like I'm gonna have to do all of the planning myself," I tell him. "We better head to the office."

I climb onto my polar bear's back.

"But on the way there," I say, leaning closer to his ear, "I need to make one quick stop."

CHAPTER 29

Miscue

"I'm looking for my father," I tell the man wearing the fedora. "He works here."

"What's his name?" the man asks.

"Dad," I answer proudly.

"That's Tom's son," says the tattooed bartender.

She turns toward me.

"Your dad's in the office. You might want to wait a minute, though. I think he's talking to somebody."

I look behind me at the closed office door.

"I hope for the sake of whomever he's talking to that they listen to him," I tell the bartender. "My father is a trained assassin."

The bartender nods. "Can I get you

something to drink while you wait?" she asks. "Maybe a Coke?"

"Whiskey, neat," I say, because it is what detectives say.

"Okay," the bartender answers. "One Coke."

"Hey, while you're back there, can I get a piece of paper and a pen?" I ask.

"Sure," she says. "If I can find one."

She hands me a pen and a napkin. "That'll have to do, I'm afraid. And here's your Coke."

"Hey," I add, "do you serve polar bears?"

"Nope," she says, shaking her head. "We don't even serve chicken wings."

I begin writing on the napkin, but it is a difficult surface to write on.

"Make sure you give that pen back to her when you're done," says the man in the fedora, staring straight ahead. "It don't belong on the bar."

I write my note and hand her back her pen. "Thanks," I tell her. "Give my best to

Frederick Crocus if you see him."

I hop off the barstool and stick the napkin on the bulletin board.

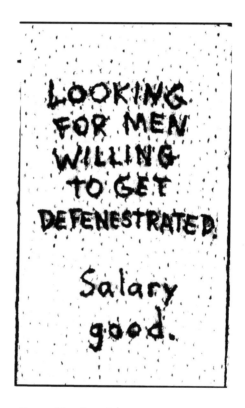

As I walk back to my barstool, I see my dad walk out of the office with an older woman who looks angry.

The woman marches out the back door of the bar.

"What are you doing here?" he asks as he approaches me.

"I came to get my script back. My film is under assault."

"Tim, that woman I was with was Ms. Dundledorf, the owner."

HER AGAIN

"What was she bugging you about?" I ask.

"You," he answers. "You, Tim. More people here were complaining about a kid being in the bar. We're lucky she didn't see you just now."

I motion for him to follow me to the pool table, where I grab a pool cue from the rack.

"What are you doing?" he asks as I hand him a second pool cue.

"This place is obviously teeming with traitors and turncoats," I tell him between gritted teeth. "We may have to fight our way out."

"Tim, this isn't some joke," says my dad.

"It's anything but a joke," I answer. "It's a crime-fighting partnership. I had intended to delay its implementation until after my film, but sometimes life just kicks you in the plans."

I climb onto the pool table and lift the stick high overhead to prepare for a brawl, and *BOOM.*

The lights go out.

Though not my lights.

The light over the pool table.

"You shattered the light!" yells my dad. "ENOUGH! DOWN! RIGHT NOW!"

I get off the pool table, now speckled with glass.

"You never LISTEN!" he shouts. Everyone at the bar stares, including the man in the fedora.

"NEVER!" repeats my dad.

"Partners don't yell at partners," I mumble.

"WHAT?" replies my dad. "WHAT did you just say?"

"We're crime-fighting partners," I tell him softly. "We're not supposed to yell at each other."

"OH, FOR GOD'S SAKE!" he barks. "I'M NOT A CRIME-FIGHTING *ANYTHING*!"

And as he shouts, he notices all the bar patrons looking at us. So he gets down on his knees and grabs my shoulder and lowers his voice.

"Tim," he says, *"I'm just a guy who works in a bar, okay? I'm just trying to make it. That's it. That's who I am. Me. That's me."*

I stare at him for a moment.

"How would I have ever known who you were?" I ask. "I barely know you."

He doesn't reply.

"So I guessed," I add. "Or maybe hoped. Though detectives rarely hope."

I lay the cue stick down on the table.

"Anyhow," I continue, "I knew when you yelled that I was wrong."

"Tim, I'm your father. And—"

"Timmy," I answer. "People call me Timmy."

"Timmy, I'm your father. And I care about you. And I don't want you to think—"

I put both my hands over his mouth. Which feels odd. Because I have never touched his face before.

But it results in a comfortable silence. Which I then break.

"Please just give me my script."

CHAPTER 30

All the News That's Fit to Hurt

When I exit the bar, my polar bear is not outside.

As it turns out, he tried to enter when he heard the yelling but could not get in due to his expired Arctic driving license.

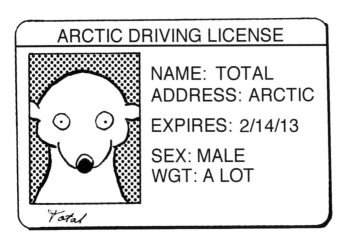

ARCTIC DRIVING LICENSE

NAME: TOTAL
ADDRESS: ARCTIC

EXPIRES: 2/14/13

SEX: MALE
WGT: A LOT

Total

So, knowing there was work to be done, Total wandered home. Where he ensconced himself in WHATT headquarters and prepared to meet his brother by sending him a faxed greeting.

And when I find him, I give him my news.

"My dad can't find my script," I tell him. "We looked everywhere, but it's not there. It's not anywhere. My film is doomed."

My bear takes a moment to digest the news.

And then hands me his.

A fax from his brother.
Which was short and to the point.

"We are in the eye of a terrible storm,"
I tell my former business associate. "This
sometimes happens."

So I sit on his lap and he holds me.

And we ride out the storm together.

CHAPTER
31
I Love the Smell of Coffee in the Morning

The next day at school is not pretty.

"So before we get started on our math problems this morning," says Mr. Jenkins, "I thought maybe we could spend ten minutes talking about the film project. How is it going?"

Tom John John stands. "Poorly, Mr. Jenkins."

"How so?" my teacher asks.

"Timmy is being difficult."

"Why? What's going on now?"

"You told us to cooperate," answers Tom John John. "And Timmy's not cooperating. He disrupts rehearsals. Harasses the actors. He won't even budge on the script. He's really not a team player, if I can be frank."

Mr. Jenkins walks over to my desk.

"Is that true, Timmy?"

"No," I answer.

"It's not?" asks Mr. Jenkins.

"Not anymore. Whatever Tom John John wants to do is fine with me."

My classmates turn their heads and stare.

"That doesn't sound like the Timmy I know," comments Mr. Jenkins.

"Yeah, well, it's the new Timmy," I reply. "Just give me whatever job you want to give me on the film. The smaller the better."

"Well, no hard feelings on my part," offers Tom John John. "I have my own script, anyway."

"And I've been helping with it," adds Scutaro. "It's quite compelling."

"Timmy," says Mr. Jenkins, "are you sure you want it to be this way?"

"Yes," I answer. "I'm sure."

"Okay, then," replies Mr. Jenkins.

"You know," adds Tom John John, "if he wants, we do have one small job available."

"What's that?" asks Mr. Jenkins.

"I need someone to bring me my coffee."

CHAPTER
32
No One Expects the Tookus Inquisition

With both the script-writing and bear-finding projects on hold, Total and I give the extra bedroom a new purpose, that of therapy room.

A place where we can commiserate.

Which we aptly call:

Or WHO for short.

But the phone won't stop ringing. For there is no rest for the hardly okay.

So I pick up the phone.

"Happy holidays from Failure, Inc.," I answer. "But we are no longer in business. So please call another detective. Whoever it is won't be as good, but tough tooties for you."

"Timmy, it's me, Rollo."

"Oh," I answer, snapping out of my professional voice. "What do you want, Rollo?"

"Sorry about calling on the Mr. Froggie

line. I didn't want to call and hear that annoying computer sound."

"Fax."

"Yeah, fax."

"The fax machine has been put away, Rollo."

"Oh. Well, I just called to see what's going on."

"With the fax machine?"

"No, not the fax machine. With you. The film. I wanted to ask you at school, but figured you didn't want to talk about it there."

I appreciate his discretion.

"The script is gone," I confess.

"Gone? What happened?"

"Foul play, I suppose. In a bar. My dad's bar."

"Your dad has a bar?" asks Rollo.

"Yes."

"He lives here?"

"Yes."

"And you met him?

"Yes."

"And—"

"For crying out loud, Rollo, what is this, the Spanish Inquisition?"

"I don't mean to ask you so many questions," says Rollo. "It's just that —"

"The point is that somebody stole the script, okay?"

"Stole it?" echoes Rollo. "Why do think that?"

"Because I left it in a bar. And bars are full of riffraff. Not to mention traitors and turncoats."

"But who would have taken it?" asks Rollo.

"I don't know."

"What do you mean you don't know? You're the detective."

"I *used* to be a detective," I tell him. "Remember?"

"Well, who was there?" he asks. "At the bar. Who did you see?"

"Does any of this really matter?"

"Yes, it matters. Who'd you see?"

"Fine. I saw Old Man Crocus there."

RESPECTED EDUCATOR

"Mr. Crocus? Our old teacher? Do you think he would steal it?"

"No. He has far too much respect for me to steal from me."

"He hated you, Timmy."

"We had professional differences, Rollo."

"Well, who else was there?"

"An elf."

"An elf?"

"The one the reindeer kicked in the head."

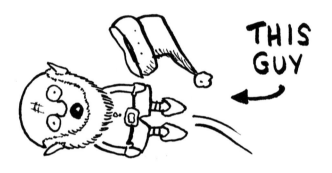

THIS GUY

"You know, I think Elmsley's fired that guy," says Rollo.

"So?"

"So maybe he had a financial motive," says Rollo.

"Great. So you're the detective now. Get

yourself a trench coat and you're all set."

"Was there anyone else suspicious?" asks Rollo.

"Just the owner."

"Who's the owner?"

"Her name is Dundledorf."

"Dundledorf," replies Rollo. "Why does that name sound familiar?"

"I have no idea, Rollo. Really. But can we stop now? This is stupid. For all I know, it was some other customer or Tom John John or Santa himself."

"It probably wasn't Santa," says Rollo. "I don't think he's a felon."

"Yeah, well, then maybe it was my dad, okay?"

Rollo pauses.

"Your dad?" he says.

I remain silent.

"You think your own dad would do something like that?" he asks.

But before I can answer, there is a knock on the office door.

CHAPTER 33

WHO's on First?

"Hi, Timmy. You working on your movie?"

"Not right now, Husband Dave."

"Well, whatever you're working on, do you mind if I check my e-mail on the computer?"

"I'm afraid I can't let you in at the moment, Husband Dave."

"You can probably just call me Dave."

"Okay, Dave."

"Listen, Timmy, I know your mom gave you the room to use. But other people get to use it also."

"Yes. But not at the moment."

"Why? What's going on in there?"

"No."

"No?" asks Dave.

"WHATT is not going on in here," I tell him. "We're closed for business."

"Who's closed for business?"

"No. WHO is open," I tell him.

"What?"

"Closed."

"Who?"

"Open."

I can tell the poor man is confused.

"I have to go now, Dave."

CHAPTER 34

Up on the Housetop, Polar Bear Claws

But the knocks on WHO's door never stop.

"Timmy," says my mother, poking her head into the room, "don't tell me you're not even dressed."

"Of course I'm dressed," I answer. "Do I look nude to you?"

NOT NUDE

"You know what I mean," she says.

"Dressed for our holiday party. Our relatives will be here any minute."

"I am not in the mood for festivities," I inform her. "Tell the holiday season to go on without me."

But she is a mother.

And so I soon look like this:

"Why are you wearing your clip-on tie?" asks my mother, never short of complaints.

"Because I don't know how to tie a tie."

"I told you Dave can help you."

"Dave doesn't know, either," I tell her.

"He does so."

"Yes, well, I tried to help him," interjects Dave as he passes us carrying a Jell-O ring. "But he wouldn't let me."

"It felt like an attempted strangulation," I reply. "I began to lose consciousness. So I defended myself."

"He did some weird karate pose," adds Dave.

But before I can answer, the doorbell rings. And I am swarmed by people in funny hats.

"Timmy! It's so nice to see you! We missed you!"

COUSIN LARRY

COUSIN MERRY

"Yes," I reply. "Greetings to you and yours. Now can I please be put back down on the floor? You're upsetting my delicate constitution."

"Did you miss us, too?" asks Larry.

"Will you put me back down if I say yes?"

"Sure."

"Then yes," I answer. "Maybe."

She puts me back down.

"Uh-oh," says her sister, my cousin Merry. "It looks like someone's standing under the mistletoe and can now be kissed."

My life thusly threatened, I flee.

And frightened and cornered, I spend the rest of the time doing a karate pose near the Christmas tree.

And then I see a chicken.

"Oh, good God!" I shout. "What fresh chaos is this? What is happening in this house? Are the holidays just an excuse for every manner of depravity?"

And then I see someone I know.

"Hiya, Timmy!"

It is Dave's nephew, Emilio Empanada, a one-time intern at my detective agency.

"Hi, Emilio."

"Sorry about the chicken," he says. "It's Edward Higglebottom the Third. Do you remember him?"

I do.

Emilio adopted him on our trip to Key West with my mom and Husband Dave last summer. And he was smaller then.

"Well, it is refreshing to see you, Emilio

SMALLER THEN

Empanada," I tell him. "For this party is filled with ravenous loons and jiggly Jell-O rings. Though I'd ask that you put your chicken on a leash. As you know, I've been attacked by one before."

MEMORIES

"Well, I don't have a leash, but I can hold him," says Emilio Empanada, lifting the chicken to his chest. "So how is the detective business?"

"I am retired," I admit. "You catch me at a particularly low moment."

"What happened?" he asks.

"If you don't mind, maybe I can tell you later. I have to go check on somebody."

"That's fine with me. I'll go say hi to Dave."

So Emilio wanders off and I wind my way through the strange people in funny hats until I get to the back door of the townhouse. And once outside, I climb the lattice that hugs the back wall.

And atop the roof, I find the other creature enduring a particularly low moment.

"Anything?" I ask.

Total shakes his head.

My former business partner has been

depressed ever since getting that fax from his brother. So to cheer him up, I told him he could wait on the roof for Santa and his reindeer, and that if the reindeer came close enough, he could eat one.

But Christmas is still a couple weeks off.

And there are no reindeer.

And even if there were, he'd probably just make friends with them.

So I put my arm around his big furry shoulder and tell him that everything is going to be okay.

And it is a moment of yuletide respite.

Shattered quickly by a cacophony of voices.

"Holy sleigh bells!" I cry. "Does this holiday offer no refuge for the weary?"

So I crawl down the front pitch of the roof and crane my head over the edge of the roof gutter, where I see something profoundly disturbing.

Two caroling snowmen.

The two of them proceed to mangle the song once known as "Hark! The Herald Angels Sing."

Making me think that there aren't any angels at all, because if there were, they would fly down from heaven and drop a tree on these two.

And when the song mercifully ends, I hear my mom say, "Thank you," and shut the front door on the snowmen.

Who then look up.

"Timmy, we came here for you."

CHAPTER
35
Four Eyes Made Out of Coal

There are many scenarios I have envisioned for how I would one day meet my end. But none of them involved a snowman.

"Are you an assassin?" I shout down from the roof.

"No," they each answer.

Reassured, I climb down from the roof and run to the front of the townhouse.

Where I quickly find that one of them is headless.

"Molly Moskins! How do you even know where I live? We just moved here."

"School directory," she says. "The school directory knows all."

"Well, what are you doing here?"

"She's here for the same reason I'm here," says the other snowman, removing its head.

Revealing not an assassin.

But worse.

CHAPTER 36
Totals We Have Heard on High

"First you sabotage my film, and now you disturb my most cherished time with relatives?" I cry to Corrina Corrina.

"You hate the holidays," says Molly. "You complain about them all the time."

"I will not be contradicted by a snowman," I tell her. "Especially a headless one."

"And you don't like your relatives, either," adds Molly.

"Okay, that's enough," I answer, spinning around and marching back toward the townhouse. "I have a refreshing eggnog waiting to be enjoyed with friends and family."

"We want to help you make your film," says Corrina Corrina.

I stop.

"Is this a joke?" I ask, looking back.

"No," she says.

"*You?* Help *me?*" I ask. "Please. Don't waste my time."

I continue toward the townhouse.

"I think I know where we can find your script," adds Corrina Corrina.

I stop on the front porch. "What do you know about my script?"

Corrina Corrina smiles. "The bar, Old Man Crocus, the angry elf. I know more than you think."

"You talked to Rollo," I say, placing my hands on my hips. "So what? He knows only what I told him. And it wasn't much."

"Yeah?" says Corrina Corrina. "Well, I know about Dundledorf."

I pause.

"What do you know?" I ask.

"She was your therapist. Your mom sent you to her. It was embarrassing and you hated it. Hated her. She didn't much like you, either. And you left a script in her bar. Right there for the taking because you didn't remember who she was. And your script disappeared."

I stare at Corrina Corrina.

"How do you know all that?" I ask.

"She's really, really splendiferously smart," says Molly. "It's impressive."

There is an awkward silence, followed by the sliding of a bear's rear end down the roof and into a rhododendron bush.

"He's having a tough month," I offer.

I turn back toward Corrina Corrina.

"Tell me one thing," I say, staring into her coal-black eyes. "Why in the name of Rudolph's red nose would you help me? You want to *destroy* me."

"Destroy you?" answers Corrina Corrina. "I mean, you annoy me, and, no, we can't afford flying elephants, but destroy you? Who has time for that? I just want to get a good grade."

"Fine," I say, pondering the twists and turns of her purported logic. "So why not just make Tom John John's film?"

"Because Tom John is more annoying than you. And more important, his climactic scene involves a five-minute kiss between you and me."

"How repugnant!" I cry.

"Yes," she says. "No offense."

"You should know that Rollo says we once kissed," I add.

"Rollo is wrong."

"Rollo is always wrong," I say.

"And excuse me," interjects Molly

Moskins, "but Tom John's script now has a five-minute kiss between you and me also. And that's very offensive. Because *I'm* the real love interest in the film, and my kiss with you should be significantly longer than *her* kiss with you. No offense, Corrina Corrina."

"None taken," she answers.

"But no matter how many times I asked," Molly continues, "Tom John refused to change his precious script. The pompous little runt."

"I see," I answer as I stare at the two headless snowwomen. "But there is one thing that still troubles me."

"What is it?" asks Corrina Corrina.

"If we are really going to join forces and find this script, it would mean I'd have to come out of retirement."

"So?"

"So the gods told me to retire. They gave me a sign."

"Can't the gods give you a new sign?" asks Molly. "One that tells you to *not* retire?"

"I suppose," I answer. "But what?"

I search my mind. And immediately think of one.

"Tomorrow. After school. Don't be late," I tell the headless snowwomen.

"What does that mean?" asks Corrina Corrina. "Are we meeting you somewhere?"

"Yes."

"Well, an address would be helpful. Because right now it could be anywhere in the world."

"Right," I answer, impressed by her attention to detail. "I'll give it to you at school."

CHAPTER 37

You Better Watch Out, You Better Not Cry, You Better Not Pout, I'm Telling You Why: Santa Claus Is Stealing Your Things

When we meet at the appointed place the following day, my fellow detectives are stunned.

"What is this place?" asks Molly Moskins.

"My secret office," I answer. "Well, one of many."

"Looks like a storage unit," says Corrina Corrina.

"Yes." I nod. "Intentionally."

I lift the large metallic door and invite them inside. "Sit on any box. They're all just props."

"Okay, Timmy," says Corrina Corrina. "The first thing I want to know is why you didn't save a copy of your script on the computer."

"I never save anything on a computer."

"Why not?"

"Russian hackers," I answer.

"Wait," she says. "So you had just one physical copy of the script and now it's gone."

"Stolen," I correct her. "By any one of three suspects. Four if you count Santa Claus."

"We probably shouldn't count Santa Claus," says Molly.

"Wrong," I tell her. "Think about it. How does he get all those gifts?"

"I don't know."

"Bingo."

"Whoa," says Molly. "That's why you're a detective and I'm not."

"So who do you see as the other suspects?" asks Corrina Corrina.

"Crocus, Dundledorf, and my father. Oh, and the elf. He may be in a criminal conspiracy with Santa Claus."

"So five, total," says Molly.

Corrina Corrina rubs her chin. "You really think your dad is a suspect? Because that seems kind of odd."

"It is. But my father is a fathomless mystery to me. So I can't count him out."

"A fathomless father," repeats Molly. "I don't even know what that means, but it sounds wonderful."

"You need to focus," I tell her.

"I'm trying," Molly says. "But it's hard with all that beeping."

I listen and hear a faint beep.

"It might be a smoke alarm," I answer.

"Are either of you smoking pipes?"

"No," answers Molly.

"Then I don't know," I tell her. "And who cares, anyway? You're supposed to be focusing on the suspects, Molly."

"Right," she answers. "Santa bad."

Corrina Corrina stands and begins pacing.

"We need to canvass the bar," she says. "Look for clues. Question witnesses. Because somebody there knows something."

"Yes," I answer. "And the two of you need to do it immediately. Before any witnesses get knocked off or the place gets burned to the ground."

"Aren't you coming with us?" asks Corrina Corrina.

"Can't. My father and I aren't on speaking terms. He knows I suspect him. And he's not happy about it."

"So we have to do this on our own?" asks Molly.

"Yes. And you'll want to blend in. So when you get there, sit at the bar and order a whiskey neat."

"Neat. What's that mean?"

"I think it's when the bartender is extra tidy."

"Okay," answers Molly. "But where is this bar?"

"Other side of town from here."

"That's far," says Molly. "Too far to walk."

"You won't be walking," I answer.

CHAPTER 38
Return to Offender

"I've never ridden one of these before!" cries Molly as I run behind her and Corrina Corrina. "It's *fast*!"

"Yes!" I answer between labored breaths. "The Segway is notoriously fast!"

Which I know because it used to be my Failuremobile.

Before my mother sold it.

Or so she said.

But the truth was that she hid it under some blankets.

In a storage unit.

Which I happened to notice when I was looking for a fax machine.

"And we have permission to use it?" asks Molly.

"Perhaps," I answer, trying to keep up with the lightning-quick vehicle.

"What does that mean?" she asks.

"Listen, Molly, when you're a detective, information like that is on a need-to-know basis."

"Well, I need to know what to say if we see your mother."

"If you see my mother, make yourself large, wave your arms around, and bang on pots and pans if you have them."

"That's what you do if you see a bear," interjects Corrina Corrina.

"There are a lot of similarities," I answer.

DEFENSE AGAINST
BEARS OR MOTHERS

I watch as the two of them turn the corner toward my father's bar. And I walk the rest of the way home by myself.

Where I find Marco the Mailman.

"Hello there, Timmy," says Marco. "You want to take the mail in for your mother?"

"Yes, Marco. I always like to see if there are any checks from clients. I have many that still owe me vast reams of cash."

"I see," he says, handing me the mail.

"No one likes a deadbeat," I add.

"No," says Marco.

I scan through the mail and see bills for my mother and catalogs for Dave.

And a letter addressed to me.

6380 Madison Ave.
San Albany, CR

TIMMY FAILURE
43 BRADBERRY ROAD
SAN ALBANY, CR

"Well, this is suspicious," I announce. "There's no name on the return address."

"So?" asks the mailman.

"So as a detective, I can tell you this is most likely a bomb."

"It would be a very thin bomb," says the mailman. "Because that envelope's no thicker than a slice of bologna."

"Yes," I answer. "It could be explosive bologna."

I make Marco stand back as I open the envelope.

And it doesn't explode.

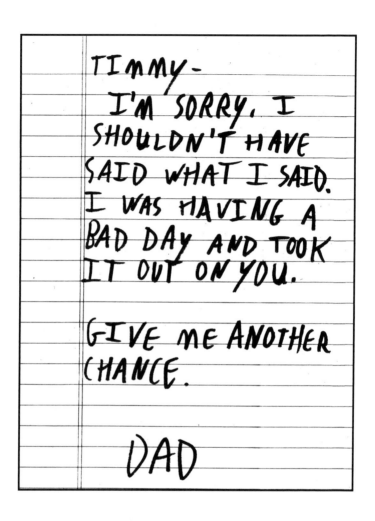

TIMMY -
I'M SORRY. I
SHOULDN'T HAVE
SAID WHAT I SAID.
I WAS HAVING A
BAD DAY AND TOOK
IT OUT ON YOU.

GIVE ME ANOTHER
CHANCE.

DAD

"Do you have a pen I can use?" I ask the mailman.

"Yeah," he says, handing me the marker clipped to his front pocket.

So I use his pen and hand him back the letter.

I head back to headquarters, which we have recently rechristened.

Or WHEN for short.

And inside I find Total.

Total sits in here every day hoping for a miracle fax to spill out of the fax machine.

One from his brother saying that he

didn't really mean it or that he's changed his mind or that he loves his little brother.

But it doesn't come.

And the days are long.

"Listen, Total, I've been thinking. Rather than give up, let's write back to your brother to see if we can change his mind."

He shakes his head.

"It's better than moping," I tell him. "What good does that do?"

But he just groans.

"Okay," I tell him. "You can at least help me find the stolen script. Maybe send some faxes for me?"

I turn on the fax machine and the error light flashes.

"What's wrong with this thing?" I ask.

So I open the top of it.

"There's a jammed piece of paper in here," I tell him. "No wonder it's not working."

So I pull out the piece of paper and go to throw it in the trash can, but the text catches my eye.

And I know immediately what it is.

"Hey, Total, stand up for a second."

But he is too pouty to move.

So I hop up on the ottoman and stare down at his protuberant belly.

"You don't have an outie! You have an innie!" I yell.

Total lifts his head.

"This is the second page of the fax you got. It just got stuck in the machine. And the guy is describing a brother who has an outie belly button. But you have an innie!"

He grabs the paper with both paws.

"Total, he's not your brother."

CHAPTER 40

I Do Not Like Tom John and Ham

The news that Total's brother is still out there to be found taxes the already strained resources of WHEN.

"We are simultaneously in search of a stolen script *and* working on a missing-person case," I tell Rollo Tookus on our walk home from school the next day.

"But we have two film rehearsals this week," argues Rollo. "One this afternoon and one on Thursday."

"Yes, that's why Molly is going to report back to me on the Thursday one and you're going to report back on today's."

SPY NUMBER ONE   SPY NUMBER TWO

Stanfurd

"But what about you?" he says. "They're gonna notice you're not there."

"Tell them I'm sick."

"But I hate lying."

"You're not lying. You're just buying me time to find my stolen script. I mean, really, what's the point of rehearsing Tom John John's script anyway? It's all gonna be for nothing when we find mine."

"It's still lying," he says.

"You'll do great," I reassure him.

But he doesn't do great.

As his report later shows:

At the rehearsal, I served my mother's honey-glazed ham lightly brushed with Dijon mustard for just the right amount of heat. Perfect for the holidays!

"Divine," said Toody Tululu.

"Made my toes tingle," said Nunzio Benedici.

Mother's Honey-Glazed Ham

Oh, and Tom John John asked where you were. Told him you were sick. He asked, "Sick how?"

Told him you had bubonic plague.

Molly's account was at least more thorough, though not without flaws.

> Today we rehearsed a new ending for the film written by Scutaro.
>
> In it, an 82-year-old Timmy dies alone in a squalid apartment surrounded by cats.
>
> It went well.

But then she tacked on this addendum:

> When rehearsal was over, Tom John John explained that the final credits will roll over a ballet number in which all of us will be dressed as flying cat angels.

Like this.

And she could not keep from editorializing.

> It was a stupid idea.
>
> As are all of his ideas.
>
> Because Tom John John is lower than mouse poop.

CHAPTER 41

Ten Tims A-Leaping

With the bar investigation safely in the hands of Corrina Corrina and Molly, I decide to head to the city library to do more research on Total's missing brother.

But with both investigations heating up, assassins lurk. So instead of exiting out the front door of our townhouse, I jump from the roof into the rhododendron bush in the front yard.

And encounter a questionable character.

"You okay?" asks my dad.

"I'm fine," I answer from within the bush.

"Can I help you?"

"I don't need any help."

I crawl out of the bush and brush off some rhododendron leaves.

"Listen, Tim—Timmy—I just came over to talk because—"

"I can't," I say as I get up and walk past him. "I have important things to do. Much more important than this."

"Just two minutes. One minute. Anything."

"You should probably go to your bar," I call back to him. "You don't want to get fired."

"Too late," he says.

I stop. And turn around.

"You got fired?"

"Yeah. And it wasn't because of you or the dumb light."

"What was it?"

"These two little girls came by looking for the script. One with a bow in her hair and one who smelled like a tangerine. Figured they were friends of yours."

"Associates."

"Associates. So I let them in to look around, and the tangerine-scented one walks right up to the bar and orders something called a . . ."

WHISKEY, TIDY.

"She was never good at following directions," I mumble.

"Anyway, Dundledorf sees the whole thing and cans me. Boom. Just like that."

I nod.

"But it'll be all right," he says. "My friend got me a part-time gig at that Kooky Kringle's tree lot down the street. Selling Christmas trees."

"And how are you doing?" he asks.

I pause before answering.

"I should probably tell you that our

investigation has uncovered a past history that I supposedly had with this Dundledorf. It's confidential, but I can tell you she had it in for us."

My dad smiles. "So she knew we were crime-fighting partners?"

I stare at him.

"No," I respond. "Nobody thinks that anymore."

I turn to walk off.

"Listen, Timmy, wait. Let me just say one thing and I'll leave you be."

"I have to go."

"Just one more minute. Really. Just one."

He sits on the front lawn beside me.

"This whole dad thing, you have to understand, I have no idea what I'm doing. None. I wasn't there when you were young. I should have been. But I wasn't. And I can't just go back and start over. You're not a baby. You're—"

"Nine."

"Nine. Nine years old. How do I make up nine years?"

I watch as he picks a few blades of grass and tosses them into the wind.

"All I can do is try," he continues. "But, Timmy, please, give me a chance to screw up. I'm new to this. And when it comes to being a father, I have a lot to learn."

I watch as the grass flutters away.

And turn back toward my dad.

"Your minute is up."

CHAPTER 42

Boy, Meats, Man

"Well, you look good," says a voice from behind me in the library conference room.

"Flo, please," I answer without looking up. "I need time to concentrate. Finding a polar bear in the Arctic is like trying to find a needle in a pancake stack."

NO NEEDLES

"Okay, that's not quite the expression, but kudos for trying."

I turn around.

"Mr. Jenkins, what are you doing here?" I ask.

"What are *you* doing here?" he replies. "I figured you were dead. Bubonic plague and all."

"Yes, well, it comes and goes," I answer, blowing my nose for effect.

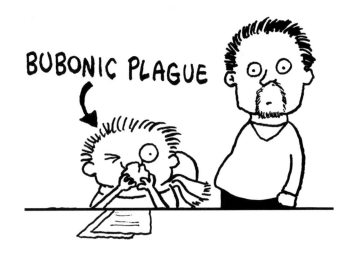

Mr. Jenkins sits down in the seat next to me.

"Listen, Timmy, Rollo's filled me in on everything."

"Who is this Rollo?"

"So I know about the missing script."

"I deny everything."

"And that you're trying to find it."

"Slander."

"And that you're still hoping to make your film."

"Lies! Fibs! Charcuterie!"

"Okay," he says. "I'm pretty sure that last one is a plate of meats."

"I'm hungry now," I conclude. "Can we finish?"

"Yep," he says. "But, Timmy, listen. I'm not gonna say anything to your mom. But you can't be missing rehearsals. Okay? Because then we will have an issue."

I say nothing.

"Oh, and one more thing," he says. "I

don't know if you're gonna find your script or whether you're gonna get to make the film you want, but, uh"—he pauses—"well, this part's sort of confidential."

He pats the underside of the table with his hands.

"What are you doing?" I ask.

"Checking for listening devices," he answers. "How do I know this place isn't wired for sound?"

"I've checked," I tell him. "I can assure you it's not."

He nods and lowers his voice.

"Anyhow, I don't know if you're gonna be able to find it or not, but I hope you do. . . ."

He looks from side to side and then lowers his voice.

"Because that Tom John John is a pain in my patootie."

CHAPTER 43

Hark! The Rollo Angel Sings

And Tom John John is a pain in my patootie as well.

Not to mention a pain in the patooties of Corrina Corrina, Nunzio, Max, Scutaro, Toody, Molly, and Rollo.

For in the rehearsals that followed, he decided to make all of us flying cat angels.

In fact, the only person who got out of it was Angel, and that is only because he threatened to throw Tom John John in a kitty litter box.

And even worse, none of us knew a thing about ballet.

But with filming only a short time away and no other script to work from, each of us had little choice but to try to learn Tom

John John's oddly named ballet poses.

And things at home are not much better.

For the beeping that Molly heard in the storage unit had more significance than I foresaw.

"Timmy, the storage rental place called and said my unit's burglar alarm went off," my mom tells me as she tucks me into bed one night. "Do you remember if we locked the door when we left?"

"Yes. No. I don't know," I answer definitively.

"Well, I couldn't remember, either, so I went down to the unit to check. And sure enough, it was unlocked."

"Oh," I say. "These things happen."

"Yeah, but then I went through all the stuff to see if anything was missing. And guess what I found out. Guess, Timmy."

It is at this point in the conversation that I want to hop into a cardboard box and ship myself to China, safe from my mother's wrath.

All because of the Segway.

You see, my logic was that my mother so rarely went to the storage locker that she would never notice it was gone. So I didn't bother to tell Corrina Corrina and Molly that they had to return it. I just figured they could ride around on it for as long as they were working on the stolen script case.

So as my mother's eyes narrow to tiny slits and her gaze bores a hole in my perspiring forehead, I know that I must confess all. My only hope: points for honesty.

"Mother, I —"

"I found the pearl necklace your great-aunt Colander gave me!" she blurts out. "I thought I had lost that thing forever!"

She holds it out for me to see.

And it is as though the governor has called to give me a death-row reprieve.

"I'm very happy for you, Mother," I say, trying not to drip sweat on her pearls. "Those are quite beautiful."

"But that's not all," she adds. "Because then I realized I had gone all the way down there and not brought the storage-unit key. Lucky for me the padlock was open, or I wouldn't have been able to get in there at all. So then I had to race back home and grab the key so I could relock it. You know, the key I always keep hanging on the refrigerator."

And suddenly, I could not remember if I had put the key back on the refrigerator.

And in a flash, it is as though the governor has called all over again.

"And guess what I saw when I went to

the kitchen," my mother says, her stare cold, causing my blood to pump like I am being strangled by an anaconda.

"Mother," I say, "I'm afraid I can't take any more of this guessing."

"Oh," she answers. "I found a Christmas card to you from—who else?—Aunt Colander! I thought you'd be thrilled. There's probably money in it. Gee, you're no fun at all."

She hands me the letter and leaves.

"Oh," she adds, pausing in the doorway, "the key was there, too."

There was no cash in my great-aunt Colander's Christmas card.

HE KNOWS WHEN YOU'VE BEEN BAD AND GOOD

But there was this little rhyme inside it:

> *Just writing to say*
> *Merry Christmas, honey.*
> *But that's all you get,*
> *'Cause I ain't got money.*
>
> CALL <u>ME</u>.

So I do.

"Well, hello, stranger," she says. "I'm surprised you remember this old lady."

"Of course I remember you," I tell my aunt. "You were Agent X, an integral part of my detective agency."

"A badge I still wear proudly," she says.

"You should. For an amateur, you showed potential."

"I will take that compliment in the spirit in which it was offered."

"Are you at home now?" I ask.

"I wish," she says. "Stupid doctors stuck me in a hospital. Been here two weeks."

"If it's against your will, I can send in a team," I tell her.

"I may take you up on that," she answers. "But for now I should probably stay put."

"Sniffles?"

"Bigger, I'm afraid."

"I understand," I tell her. "I, myself, have been struggling with bubonic plague."

"Is that so?" she asks.

"Affirmative," I answer.

There is a pause, followed by the sound of her talking to someone.

"Sorry about that," she says. "Nurses won't leave me alone."

"I am constantly hounded by the outside world," I respond. "So I am sympathetic."

"Yes, well, I'm afraid I'm one of those people hounding you at the moment, so I don't want to keep you. But before I go, one quick thing."

"You need a job?"

"Oh, well, no. But the subject matter is probably just as bothersome."

"What?"

"I hear you've been talking to your father," she answers.

"How do you know that?"

"Your mom told me."

"That woman gossips like a caffeinated crow."

CAW CAW CAW CAW CAW

My aunt laughs. Then coughs.

"Don't make me giggle," she says. "Hurts too much."

I wait for her to stop coughing.

"Anyhow," continues my aunt, "I don't think your mom knows what to say to you about it."

"What does that mean?"

"Well, you never had a dad in your life. And now suddenly you do. He sort of surprised you by appearing out of nowhere, didn't he?"

"Yes," I offer. "Like a cougar in a peach tree."

"Well, I've never heard that expression before, but sure, I suppose it works."

She coughs again.

"The point, Timmy, is that your mom thinks this is all sort of up to you. Whether you want to spend time with him. Or whether you don't."

"Yes, well, I don't," I say. "So problem solved."

"Right," she answers. "You were always good at solving problems."

"I'm a professional," I tell her. "At everything I do."

"Of course," she says. "Speaking of which, did you know that your dad once wanted to be a writer for a living? Not sure if it's still the case. But it was."

"How do you know that?"

"I used to know him. Briefly. Back when he was with your mother. Big dreamer. Not a bad guy. Just young."

"No," I reply. "He's mostly bad."

She laughs again. Then groans.

"All right, I'm gonna let you go back to your work," she says. "I don't want criminals thinking they can run amok."

"Won't happen," I assure her.

"Hey, final thing, Timmy."

"What's that?"

"Forgive people sometimes. Even if you don't think they deserve it. Because one day *you* won't deserve it. And someone will surprise you and do the same."

"Like a cougar in a peach tree," I answer.

"Sure," she says. "Or maybe more like a beautiful butterfly landing on your head."

"I loathe butterflies."

LOATHE THEM

"Okay," she says. "Cougar in a peach tree."

"I'm glad we agree."

She coughs. Much harder this time.

"Okay, sweetheart," she says. "I'm signing off. I love you, I love you, I love you. And if there's a big blue place where they let me roam around after this, well, then, I'll love you from there as well."

"Ditto," I answer.

"Good-bye, love."

CHAPTER 45

High Pane Tolerance

When I hang up the phone, I am greeted by a loon in the windowpane.

"Molly, you're two stories up!" I cry. "What do you think you're doing?"

"You said assassins expect conventional entries and exits. And I don't want to die."

"Well, you might now," I inform her. "Why are you disturbing me in my abode?"

"Big news," she says. "Corrina Corrina wants to meet."

"Where?" I ask.

"Her detective headquarters."

"That big bank downtown?"

"No," she answers.

"She's in a new office now," Molly continues. "One you've never seen. At least, not from the inside."

"Well, climb down," I tell her. "And don't break your head. I'll meet you in the backyard."

"Okay," she says.

"Hey, and Molly?" I call out to her as she begins climbing down. "What's the big news?"

Molly looks up at me and smiles, her mismatched pupils dancing in the December sun.

"She found your script."

CHAPTER 46

The Man Who Moved Too Much

Molly and I race to Corrina Corrina's office like sharks to a chum-fest.

And as we run, I pepper her with questions.

"So how did she find it? Where was it? What happened?"

"Timmy, we're almost there," says Molly, running ahead of me. "And you always say we have to be careful about security. There are spies *everywhere*."

I stop suddenly. She does the same.

"Good point," I answer. "So speak in code."

"But I don't know any code."

"Just say it backward."

"Okay. Corrina Corrina and I went back to your dad's bar a second time."

"What are you doing?" I ask.

"Saying it backward," she says.

"No, Molly Moskins! Say your *words* backward!"

"Oh, this is way too confusing," she replies. "I'm just gonna say it!"

"Then say it already!" I cry.

"Corrina Corrina and I went back to your dad's bar a second time. And the mean lady wasn't there."

"Dundledorf?"

"Right. So Corrina Corrina was able to talk to people. And once she started asking questions, she found out it was Crocus—"

"Just as I suspected," I announce. "I knew it all along."

"No. She found out it was Crocus who was staring at us from the other side of the bar. It was a little hard to see him at first."

"Please don't pause mid-sentence like that."

"Well, don't interrupt," she says. "Anyway, she walked toward Crocus and he was very nice to her. But then, she saw that elf. And knew instantly that it was him—"

"Just as I suspected," I announce. "I knew it all along."

"No, Timmy. It was him, the same guy who got kicked by the reindeer."

"This is very hard to take, Molly! Please stop pausing in the middle of your words."

"I'm not. You just keep talking over me! Anyhow, in the middle of our talking to the elf, your dad walks back in, I guess to get his last check. And, well, he confessed—"

"Just as I suspected," I announce. "I knew it all along."

"No, Timmy! Confessed that he hadn't been very nice to you and said he felt bad."

"OH, THIS IS UNBEARABLE!" I shout. *"Molly, do not pause between your words like that!"*

"I'm not pausing! You just keep jumping in! The point is that this old man in a fedora walked over to us and revealed everything!"

"Oh, great, so let me guess—he revealed to Corrina Corrina that he didn't like beer? Revealed that he didn't want the television so loud? Revealed that he wasn't fond of little kids yammering in the bar? Tell me, Molly, what stupid scenario is it *this time?*"

Molly just stares at me.

"He revealed to Corrina Corrina that you left the script on the bar that day. And it didn't belong there. So he put it behind a stack of phone books under the bar."

She twirls her finger through her curls.

"Anyhow, that's where Corrina Corrina found it."

Astonished, I am unable to speak.

"Gee," she says, "why can't you always be this quiet?"

CHAPTER 47

Just Fall on Your Nose

Focused but famished, we make a brief stop at a taco truck.

"Molly, under my guidance, you have done fine work," I tell her. "I shall reward you with a tasty taco."

"Four tasty tacos," she says.

"It's unfortunate to see you take advantage of my generosity."

"But I'm hungry."

"I will buy you one tasty taco," I tell her, purchasing it from the man in the truck and handing it to her.

She takes a large bite out of it, and with lettuce and cheese falling from her mouth, says this:

"Oh, I forgot to tell you the bad news."

"Bad news?" I ask. "What bad news?"

"The script. Mostly blank."

"What are you talking about?"

"Your script. The pages didn't have words on them."

"Molly Moskins, that script was a two-hundred-fifty-page cinematic masterpiece."

"Yeah, well, only two of the pages had words on them," she says, salsa dripping from the corner of her mouth. "Something about your birth and a bunch of flying elephants. And then, nada. Hey, could I get a burrito with this?"

"Molly Moskins, you obviously left some of the script pages at the bar!"

She burps.

"Nope."

"What do you mean, 'nope'? How do you know?"

"Because you numbered the pages. And there they all were, pages one to two hundred fifty."

"But how can you possibly explain all those blank pages?" I ask. "That makes no sense."

"That confused Corrina Corrina also. But that's the part *I* figured out."

"Figured it out how?"

"Well, remember how you told everyone you worked on the script all night? That made you very sleepy. So at some point in the early morning, you drifted off. And, boom, your nose hit the delete key and wiped out the last two hundred forty-eight pages."

"Wiped them out?" I cry.

"Indeed," she answers.

"You mean my schnozz caused all this?"

"Yep. In fact, the scientific name for it is *Fallasleep-schnozzo-deletus*. It's a known malady."

"Well, I must admit I have no medical

background. And I *have* had bubonic plague lately."

"Yes," answers Molly. "One leads to the other."

She wipes her mouth across her forearm.

"Anyhoo, you didn't notice what you had done, and so you woke up in the morning and just pressed print. Didn't bother to go through the printed pages. Didn't bother to save a copy on the computer."

"The Russians," I say. "They steal everything."

"Yeah, well, whatever your reason, the work was—"

She pauses to swallow the last bite of her food.

"Gone," she says. "Just like that taco."

"Molly Moskins, I should hold you upside down and shake that last taco out of you."

ARTIST'S INTERPRETATION

THE SUNDAY TIMES

Elf loses lawsuit

SHAKE
SHAKE
SHAKE

THE
SUNDAY
TIMES

"Please don't," she says. "I'd hate to catch your *Fallasleep-schnozzo-deletus*. And besides, there's Corrina Corrina's building."

CHAPTER 48

Movin' On Up to a Deluxe Detective Headquarters in the Sky

From the earliest days of my agency, my goal was to locate my headquarters on the top floor of the highest building in town.

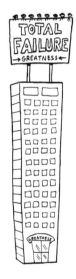

From high atop my perch, I would look out through that blue-green glass and scan the cityscape for wrongdoers and miscreants.

And I would know what it was like to be the most successful detective in the world at the height of his power.

And now I did.

"Your dad *owns* this building?" I ask Corrina Corrina.

"I think he just rents the top three floors. I'm not really sure. But when he has to meet someone in the office on the ground floor, he lets me come up here and play."

"You don't mean 'play,'" I tell her. "You mean do your detective work."

"Right," she says.

I take a seat at an empty desk.

"I told Timmy what happened," says Molly. "About finding the script and it being blank and all."

The leather seat reclines.

"Yeah, Timmy," says Corrina Corrina. "I'm afraid we're really in trouble without a script. And at such a late date, we don't have many options."

I open a desk drawer and find pencils.

"So I was thinking," says Corrina Corrina. "Maybe we just go into Mr. Jenkins's office before school tomorrow and tell him everything that happened. Just be honest."

"Yeah," adds Molly. "Maybe we can get

an extension or something. Or maybe he can get Tom John John to compromise."

"Which he probably won't," adds Corrina Corrina.

"Timmy, you're barely talking," says Molly.

I stare at Molly from behind the desk.

"Tell the polar bear to meet me in the underground garage," I announce. "We have a script to write."

CHAPTER 49

We Tree Kings of Orient Are

"Kooky Kringle is frightening," I tell my polar bear. "He looks emotionally unstable."

"Coming through," says a man with a tree overhead. "Could you just move a bit to the side?"

And when I turn, he sees that it is me.

"Timmy!" says my dad. "What are you doing at the Christmas-tree lot?"

"I'm studying the facial features of Kooky Kringle. I suspect he's a felon. Or perhaps the victim of a nuclear disaster."

"Yeah, well, maybe," says my dad. "So that's why you came here?"

"Partly," I answer. "But also because I heard you write. Or used to."

He laughs. "Who told you that?"

"Confidential," I answer.

"Okay, well, yes. Years ago. Nothing serious. I really wasn't very good. Why?"

"Pardon me," says a customer to my dad. "Can we get a tree stand on that?"

"For sure," answers my dad. "Give me one second."

My dad looks back toward me.

"Why do you want to know if I write?"

"Because we need to do a film script. And it needs to be astoundingly great. Perhaps genius."

He laughs again. "Okay. I mean, I don't know if I ever tried doing a film script, but it sounds fun. When do you want to do it?"

"We need to start tonight. Or we are most likely doomed."

"Well, I can't do it tonight, Timmy. I mean, we're a little busy."

We stare at each other, flanked on either side by Christmas trees.

An older man pokes his head between two of the trees.

"Tom, are you gonna put that stand on that guy's Christmas tree? He's just standing there by his car."

"Yeah, I am," my dad says. "Timmy, you're just gonna have to excuse me. I'm sorry. We'll do it. But another night, okay?"

I watch as my father jogs off toward the customer.

As kids and their parents walk past me.

And I stand there.

Wishing I could slip between the trees and disappear.

And then I feel a hand on my shoulder.

"I told him he could probably put on his own Christmas-tree stand," says my dad. "And he wasn't happy about it."

He scratches the side of his face.

"Do you know if anyone in this town is hiring?"

I smile at him.

"Thanks," I say.

I hold out my hand to shake his.

"A handshake?" he asks. "A little formal. How about a hug?"

"Too soon," I tell him.

We shake hands.

And as we walk off the tree lot, I look around to find my bear.

And find him still staring at the poster bearing the image of Kooky Kringle.

Only he's not staring at Kooky Kringle.

CHAPTER 50

He Ain't Heavy

When Total and I get home, we head straight for our headquarters, newly christened with a holiday-themed name:

Wishing YOU A Happy Yuletide

Inside the locked room, Total unrolls the poster he has torn off the wall of Kooky Kringle's.

And points.

And I immediately understand.

"It's your brother."

He nods.

And after just a few hours of research and a dozen faxes, we find him.

And he contacts us.

And as it turns out, Total is not the only polar bear who has been waiting a long time for this.

> I've been looking my whole life for you, little brother.

"That's the problem with our chosen profession," I tell my polar bear. "We were living incognito. Impossible to track."

Total nods.

In his fax, his brother also explained that after a brief career in modeling (hence, the poster) and a stint as a writer for an outdoors magazine, he went on to receive a degree in climate science from the Massachusetts Institute of Technology and was currently living in a Queen Anne Victorian home in Somerville, Massachusetts.

"Not bad for a polar bear," I comment. "Not as glamorous as your life, but still, it's something."

But Total's favorite part of the fax was the last couple lines, which simply said:

> I have an extra bedroom here that you can live in. I don't want to be apart from you another day.

"This Somerville place could be exceedingly dangerous," I warn him. "Maybe you shouldn't go."

But I can see how he is staring at the letter.

"Well, maybe you should just go for a short visit," I tell him. "And come right back."

But then he looks at me. And I know.

And I put my arm around him. And he puts his arm around me.

Two partners in crime-fighting.

Both lost for so long.

Both ready to be whole.

CHAPTER 51

So I Want to Be a Piggyback Rider

"That scene is much too sad," I tell my father in the park as we work on our film script together. "It has no *joie de vivre.* That's French for 'ducks.'"

"Ducks?" he says. "What are you talking about?"

"What are *you* talking about?" I answer.

And so it goes.

Arguing as only two professional writers can do.

For hours.

Until suddenly interrupted by a park dweller.

"Hiya, Timmy!" says Rollo.

"Rollo Tookus," I answer, "can't you see that I'm currently being visited by the screenwriting muse? There's greatness flowing through my very fingers as we speak."

"Oh," he answers. "I just saw you sitting here and thought you might want to play Frisbee with us. I'm here with my dad."

"And I'm here with mine," I tell him.

Rollo stares.

"You're Timmy's dad?"

"I am," he answers, shaking Rollo's hand. "And you're not interrupting anything. We're just butting heads."

"Wow," says Rollo. "I never thought I'd meet you. I'm Timmy's best friend."

"Yeah," answers my dad. "Timmy talks a lot about you."

"I tell him you're very smart," I add. "But also that you have an unnatural obsession with grades."

"It's true," Rollo tells my dad. "I want to go to Stanfurd."

Rollo points to his sweatshirt.

"If I go to Stanfurd, I can get a good job and not have to sell oranges by the side of the highway."

"Well, that's a good goal," says my dad. "Wish I'd gone to a good school like that. When I was young, I was too busy having a good time, if you know what I mean."

We both just stare at him.

"Okay, time for me to go get a beer from the car," he says.

"Nice to meet you, Mr. Failure," says Rollo.

"Nice to meet you, too," says my dad.

Rollo turns back to me. "So you sure you don't want to play?"

"Can't," I tell him. "We have to get this script finished."

"The script!" exclaims Rollo. "I can't believe I didn't tell you!"

"Tell me what?"

"At the last rehearsal, Tom John John got frustrated with all of us not being able to do ballet poses."

"So?"

"So he started yelling and got out of his chair and tried showing us all how to do them."

"And, boom, he broke his big toe!"

"So what does that mean?" I ask.

"I think it means he can't come to school for a few days."

"It's a sign from the gods!" I shout. "He can't interfere with my film!"

"That's what I thought," says Rollo. "But then he announced he was going to just direct the movie from home via Skype."

"So he *can* interfere with my film!"

"No!" Rollo answers. "Because then his father got transferred to Bulgaria!"

"It's a sign from the gods!" I shout.

"Yeah, and he leaves immediately."

"I shall escort him to the airport if need be," I declare. "Though someone should warn the Bulgarians that he's coming."

"Yeah," Rollo answers. "So write some good stuff. I'm gonna go play with my dad."

When my dad comes back, he has a beer can in his hand. His sits on the picnic table beside me and holds out the open can.

"Ever tasted beer?" he asks.

"No," I answer. "I only drink whiskey. Neat."

And as we sit there, I watch Rollo bouncing on his father's shoulders, his weight almost drilling his father into the soft grass.

"We should challenge them to a father-and-son race," I tell my dad.

"Like a piggyback race?"

"Yes. And perhaps wager."

My father gets up off the table and kneels on the grass. "Here, hop on."

"Well, put your beer down first."

"I can do both."

"You're violating a number of health and safety standards."

"Stop worrying so much. Hop on."

So I get on his back. And we practice.

And because he is holding only one of my legs, I start to slip off.

And he tries to catch me without spilling his beer.

And this happens:

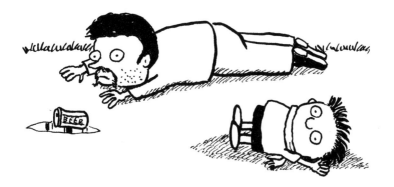

"You have broken my spleen, my skull, and my aorta," I mutter.

"Sorry," he says. "I thought I could do it."

"The good news is that I'm already implanted in the ground," I answer. "Which should save you a bundle on funeral arrangements."

"Well, that's good to hear," he says.

"You're a very imperfect father," I tell him.

"Yes," he answers. "Mistakes were made."

CHAPTER 52
Mother, Do You Think They'll Like This Film?

On the day of the film screening, I am hounded by my many fans.

"Timmy, how long are you going to take in there?" yells my mother through the closed door. "It starts in a half hour!"

"Please, Mother. I may have to walk down a red carpet. I need to look professional."

"Well, look professional faster," she says. "We're gonna be late. And Dave would like to check his e-mail before we go."

So I have two minutes of peace. Followed by a second interruption from Dave.

"You almost done, Timmy?"

"No, Dave."

"All right, fine. I'll just wait at the door."

"Please don't rush me, Dave."

I hear him whistling outside the door.

"Looks like you got a new sign," he says. "What did this used to say?"

"WHEN," I answer through the door.

"Before you put this up."

"I just told you."

"Told me what?"

"I did not say WHATT."

"Timmy, I'm just saying that now you have a new sign."

"WHY."

"Because there used to be a different one!"

"WHEN."

Then there is only silence.

Followed by the sound of Dave banging his head into the wall.

"Timmy, come out of there right now," barks my mother.

So I do.

And I look stupendous.

"What are you doing?" she asks.

"I believe this is the Hollywood look."

"Well, it's too late to change now," she says. "But you're not taking that," she says, grabbing the pipe.

So with that small adjustment, we head for Dave's car.

Where she sits in the backseat with me.

"What are you doing?" I ask. "You always sit in the front seat."

"True, but I've never been famous before," she says. "And when the flashbulbs go off, I want to be right there by your side."

"I suppose that's acceptable," I answer. "As you were there for the tough times."

"I was," she says. "I remember them well."

CRASHED CAR INTO BUILDING

BROKE PRINCIPAL'S WINDOW

She puts her arm around me.

"And I was proud of you every step of the way," she says.

"*Every* step?" I ask.

ARRESTED IN CHICAGO

"Okay," she answers. "Sometimes you made me want to pull my hair out and cry."

I nod. "I can have that effect on people."

She pulls me closer to her.

"You know," I tell her, "I plan on pursuing my Hollywood career with great vigor. And there is a good chance I will need a personal assistant. Would you be interested?"

"How is the pay?" she asks.

"Not good," I answer. "But the benefits are tremendous. One of which is that you get to spend time with a professional such as me."

She laughs and rests her forehead against the side of my head.

And blows in my ear.

Something she sometimes does to make me laugh.

"That is no way to treat a professional," I tell her.

So she stops.

"Do it again," I say.

CHAPTER 53

Greatness on Two Shoes:
The Timmy Failure Story

The film itself was a cinematic triumph.

Despite the limitations.

For as it turns out, Corrina Corrina's statements regarding the $900 budget were accurate.

So Mr. Jenkins suggested we film the entire thing in a classroom using wooden cutouts for the sets.

And because so many of the actors I wanted were unavailable, Mr. Jenkins suggested we use wooden cutouts for the characters as well, each of which was held aloft by a student.

And each of which was designed by me.

With the exception of Molly Moskins, who insisted on playing herself and wearing her eclipse glasses.

But she was much too large for the set, so

she looked like King Kong terrorizing a small town.

And she couldn't see. So that created its own problems.

TRIP

And with the absence of Tom John John, we were short a director. So Flo filled in, and cleaned up quite nicely for the premiere.

And for the most part, the film contained my entire story.

I say "for the most part" because the film's birth sequence had to be shortened to just one pathetic shot of a flying elephant.

And there was no scene with my polar bear chasing our principal off a cliff.

That was nixed by Flo.

Which wasn't so bad, except for the fact that he replaced it with a scene where the two characters have a minor disagreement over a milkshake.

But other than that, it faithfully recounted my story, including my meteoric rise to CEO of the world's largest detective agency, Failure, Inc.

An empire that contained a Timmy blimp, a Timmy ship, and a Timmy fortress.

And, over Flo's objection, I made sure that each scene was separated by a blank screen.

Onto which I flashed one word:

GREATNESS

    And through it all, Total and I vanquished our enemies, culminating in the film's much-talked-about bar scene, which was the only other scene where I had to make a few small compromises.

Such as:

And:

Though, in the end, I still did fall out of a tenth-story window. Which should have been the end of Timmy.

Except for the fact that there was one more small compromise.

And when the last scene ended, there was this brief message:

The students of Carverette wish to thank Tom John John for his contributions to the film.

To which I later added:

> **Which weren't much, because most of his ideas were weird. And now he is annoying Bulgarians.**

And a dedication:

> **In memory of the esteemed Frederick Crocus, who's not dead yet, but will be one day.**

And at the end of the credits, there was a summary of each character's life.

Like that of Molly Moskins:

Became millionaire eye model and owner of tangerine-scented perfume line.

And Corrina Corrina:

Became first female president of the United States.

Later impeached.

And Rollo Tookus:

Graduated from Stanfurd University with perfect GPA. Never had to sell oranges by the side of the highway.

Good guy.

And my own, which I tried to keep modest:

Personified greatness.

And that left only one character's ending.

CHAPTER
54
Pictures of You

When we get home after the film, I find my polar bear on the front step of the townhouse.

"You can't leave three days before Christmas!" I tell him. "My Christmas break is just starting. And we haven't even held your retirement party!"

But he doesn't answer.

And I can see by the way his paws are wrapped around his tiny suitcase that my protest is for nothing.

Because it's time for my bear to go to his brother.

And if he wants to get there in time to spend the first of many Christmases with him, he's gonna have to leave now.

Because no train would take a dangerous polar bear.

And no plane seat could fit him.

So to get there, he is going to have to rely on the same network of Goodwill trucks that the polar bears use to pick up our discarded fax machines.

"At least wait here," I tell him. "I have something for you."

So I run into the townhouse and return with a handful of gifts.

"Consider this your official retirement party," I tell him, handing him a small box.

Which he opens.

To find a watch.

"I found your size," I tell him, wrapping it around his wrist. "And maybe with enough practice, you can learn to tell time."

He smells the watch, checking to make sure it's not edible.

"And I got you a Total Failure, Inc., tie," I tell him. "That way you'll always look professional."

"Plus, it's a clip-on," I tell him. "So you can just attach it to your fur."

"Oh, and I owe you a pension," I tell him. "One seal a month for the rest of your life. But give me a few weeks on that. There aren't as many seal distributors in Somerville as I thought."

He drools.

"Oh," I tell him. "And I can't let you go without giving you a farewell speech. It's what all the professionals do."

I take out my prepared speech.

"You might want to sit back down on the

porch," I tell him. "It's not long, but I think the guest of honor always sits."

He sits back down on the porch.

"'Dearest Total,'" I begin. "'You were a brave and noble bear.'"

I hold out my hand.

"This is where we shake hands," I tell him.

He shakes my hand.

"'You served my agency with honor and distinction,'" I continue. "'You were a fearless warrior. And you were a tireless—'"

I am interrupted by the sound of squeaky brakes.

It is the Goodwill truck, here to pick up Total.

"He's here *already*?" I ask my bear. "What time was he supposed to come?"

Total looks at his watch. But he can't tell time.

The driver honks the horn.

"We're in the middle of our retirement ceremony!" I yell. "Can't you even wait?"

But I already know from Total that he cannot. The network of polar bear drivers keeps an extremely tight schedule.

So I look at my bear. And he looks back at me.

And for the first time in all the time I have known him, I see a tear roll down his furry cheek.

So I leap into his arms.

"Forget the speech!" I tell him. "Forget the stupid speech! You were my best friend. You were my best friend ever! And you saved me. You saved me from everything and everyone!"

The driver honks the horn again.

"Wait, wait, wait," I plead with Total. "Before you go, I got you one more thing."

I hold out a scrapbook.

"It's filled with pictures," I tell him. "Pictures of me and you."

"Your brother has a lot of catching up to do. And I want him to know you. I want him to know everything about you."

Total takes the scrapbook from me and puts it in his suitcase.

And the truck driver honks again.

"You gotta go," I tell him. "I know you gotta go."

He stands, suitcase in hand.

And then puts it back down.

And with both paws, he lifts me up.

"I love you," I tell him. And he presses the side of his furry cheek to mine.

And he puts me down.

And he is gone.

CHAPTER
55
The Little Rummer Boy

There's not much to tell you about Christmas.

Except that it was a sunny day.

And the first Christmas I had ever spent with my dad.

Who even gave me a gift.

Though it was odd.

"A book on how to make mixed drinks?" I ask. "You know I'm only nine, right?"

"It's for when you're older," he says.

But it was the first Christmas gift he had ever given me. So I put it above my bed.

And it was the first holiday season I had ever spent with Husband Dave.

Now just Dave.

So I got him something.

"Have one week of exclusive access!" I told him. "My office is all yours."

I could see Dave wanted to ask me questions, like *how* I had come up with the idea.

But he didn't.

And as for my mother, I got her a very special gift.

"You take it out when I'm making your head hurt," I told her. "And it erases one Timmy-induced headache."

And, filled with apple pie, the three of us spent the rest of a lazy Christmas afternoon watching movies.

Until I heard an odd sound coming from the office.

And knew it was the fax machine.

So I ran in there just in time to see a piece of paper sliding out of the machine.

And knew immediately that it was from my polar bear.

Who, with the help of his educated brother, was now a much better writer.

Dear Timmy,
 Hi.
I may be far away. But I'm with you always. Right there in the center of your heart.

LOVE, Total